A SLICE OF CHRISTMAS MAGIC

A.G. Mayes lives in Minnesota with her husband and two dogs. She loves to eat pie and this now counts as research! The Magic Pie Shop is a sweet, heartwarming and romantic series about a young woman, Susanna, whose eccentric Aunt Erma mysteriously disappears, leaving Susanna to look after her small town pie shop and mischievous dog, Mitzy.

AG_Mayes
agmayeswriter
AGMayesAuthor
agmayes.com

Also by A. G. Mayes

A Slice of Magic

A SLICE OF CHRISTMAS MAGIC

A. G. Mayes

OneMoreChapter

One More Chapter
a division of HarperCollins*Publishers*
The News Building
1 London Bridge Street
London SE1 9GF

www.harpercollins.co.uk

This paperback edition 2019

First published in Great Britain in ebook format by
HarperCollins*Publishers* 2019

A catalogue record for this book
is available from the British Library

ISBN: 9780008319144

This novel is entirely a work of fiction.
The names, characters and incidents portrayed in it are
the work of the author's imagination. Any resemblance to
actual persons, living or dead, events or localities is
entirely coincidental.

Set in Birka by Palimpsest Book Production Ltd,
Falkirk Stirlingshire

Printed and bound by CPI Group (UK) Ltd, Croydon, CR0 4YY

MIX
Paper from
responsible sources
FSC™ C007454

For Chris
and everyone who loves
pie, puppies, and magic

Prologue

From the outside, the cottage nestled in the snowy countryside at the bottom of a hill looked as if it belonged on the pages of a storybook, but for the Drake family inside life was no happily ever after.

Dennis and Stan, father and son, were playing chess by the fire when a woman with graying brown hair and sharp green eyes stormed in and threw back the hood of her cloak. The younger man felt all the muscles in his body tense.

"Did you get it?" she asked.

"No," Stan answered quietly. Dennis stared at the board.

"What?" she asked sharply. Both men flinched. "We would be in control of all the magic in Hocus Hills by now if you two blundering buffoons didn't fail at every little task." She spoke as though all the magical residents in the town of Hocus Hills were just objects for her to possess.

"We thought Alice was our star, but then she set us back when she got caught. I should have never let her convince me she could control people through altered magic spices. She didn't have the skills. I mean, cookies? Come on!" She rolled her eyes. "I don't think her heart was in the mission. She was too distracted by the loss of her sister, Nellie."

Sometimes his mother just liked to hear the sound of her own voice, Stan thought.

"We can try something else," Dennis offered, not taking his eyes off the chess board.

"Of course, we'll try something else," Brenda snapped. "We need to figure the magic out. Only two days before Ivan gets here. *Two!*" She slammed her hand on the table and chess pieces bounced off the board, clattering to the floor. "He's not as kind as I am."

"We have a plan for getting new recruits," Stan said, his voice barely above a whisper.

"We need more than your plans. We need more people before Ivan gets here. That part shouldn't be hard though. There's always magical people who want more than to hide out in a small town."

She paced up and down the room, her shoes clicking sharply against the floor. Stan watched his mother pace.

"Erma, she's always a problem. She's been keeping those spices under lock and key," Brenda was muttering under her breath now. "But think of how happy Ivan would be if we got her magic."

She went to the fireplace and threw in a couple of logs. Sparks flew, and heat poured out as the flames rose higher.

"We need the rest of them." She flung her hand at the spice bottle displayed on the mantel of the fireplace like a trophy. "You two can't get anything done right. I'll go out in the morning and sneak into the kitchen of her pie shop while she's getting ready to open. She'll have the spices out then."

"What about her niece?" Stan watched the fire instead of his mother as he asked the question.

"I think I can take her," Brenda said sarcastically.

"They still have the protection spells on the pie shop. You won't be able to use your magic," Dennis said.

She rolled her eyes. "I don't need magic. I just need to be smarter than them. That shouldn't be hard."

Brenda pulled up the hood on her cloak, threw open the door, and was gone without another word.

Dennis bent down to pick up the chess pieces and the two of them got back to their game.

Chapter 1

Dear Elodie,

My husband and I are expecting our first child in six weeks. He recently informed me that he won't be able to make it to the birth because of a "work trip". Elodie, I am beside myself. When I ask him if he can reschedule this work trip, he says those are the only days the clients are available. I find that a little hard to believe. I would think any client would understand rescheduling a business trip to be there when your baby is born. We both love our jobs, but I sometimes feel like my husband uses his as an excuse to treat me badly. What do I do?

Sincerely,
Lonely Delivery

Dear Lonely Delivery,

My recommendation would be to go back in time and have a baby with someone else. Assuming that's not a valid option, you should try to sit your husband

5

down and have an open talk about your needs right now. He may be experiencing anxiety surrounding the birth. Now I completely agree that it shouldn't be your job to soothe his nerves since you're kind of busy growing a human, but sometimes life throws these curve balls at us. Tell your husband what you told me about using his job as an excuse. Try to keep your conversation productive and avoid accusations.

And congratulations on your first child!

Ask and I'll Answer,

Elodie

I wiped a bead of sweat off my forehead with the back of my hand and surveyed the display case. It was packed full of pies. Only ten minutes until we opened.

Aunt Erma came out from the kitchen carrying a blueberry pie, her specialty. She wore a hat with felt antlers and jingle bells.

"What do you think? Do we have enough?" She stood next to me.

"Not if business keeps up the way it has," I said. We'd sold out every day this week. Now that Aunt Erma was back and could teach me her secret recipes with her magic spices, customers had been pouring through the door.

She kept her spices under magical lock and key except when we were baking. As we still had a few pies to top off with a sprinkle of spice, the wooden box was sitting on the kitchen island. It was painted purple and covered in a glittery glaze with twelve glass bottles inside. Each one was labeled with a number written in green. Bottle number three looked a little different from the rest. That was the spice Alice had stolen, and the original bottle was still missing. Aunt Erma had replaced the bottle when she'd created a new batch.

The garbage can in the kitchen was overflowing so I wheeled it towards the back door, grunting as I tried to pull it into the alley without tipping it over. I took a deep breath and heaved the plastic bag out of the bin. A "meow" startled me and I dropped the bag. It burst open and garbage spilled at my feet. I held my breath as I made eye contact with a blue-eyed cat peering at me from behind the dumpster.

Just one month ago, before I knew anything about magic, Aunt Erma had been the cat in the alley. An evil woman named Alice had turned her into a cat and stolen Aunt Erma's magic spices before opening a cookie shop and attempting to alter Aunt Erma's magic spices so she could use them to control people. She was working with Stan, the pie shop's former delivery man, and Stan's parents, Brenda and Dennis Drake. Only Alice had been caught so far, and she was in some kind of magical jail. The exact details about what exactly was involved in magical lockup were still a little fuzzy to me, and no one seemed eager to fill me in. The Drakes were still on the loose, and they had escaped with one of the bottles of magic spice. A fact that had kept Aunt Erma and I feeling a little on edge the past few weeks no matter how much we tried to focus on our holiday pie preparation.

"Meow once if you're human," I said in a low voice. The cat meowed again, and my eyes widened.

"Are you talking to a cat?" Henry asked, appearing from around the corner. His brown eyes twinkled, and his wavy brown hair stuck out from under his dark green stocking cap. Henry was my almost boyfriend. We had been dating for a few weeks, and I think we were nearing that point in the relationship when I could begin to use the B word.

"How do you know this isn't a person?" I asked, greeting him with a quick kiss.

"I'm magic," he said with a smile. "And I know that's Mrs. Peterson's cat. He likes to do a lap around town every morning."

I leaned in for another kiss, enjoying the giddy feeling of being in a new relationship.

"I have to go," Henry said, sneaking in one more kiss. This time lingering for an extra moment before pulling away. "I'm in charge of the bingo game today, and I'll never hear the end of it if I'm late." Henry worked at the nursing home. "Do you need help cleaning this up before I go?" He motioned to the pile of garbage. The breeze had begun to carry some bits across the pavement, and if I didn't clean it up quickly I was at risk of being ticketed by Sheriff Buddy for littering.

"No, no, I've got it. I don't want to be responsible for keeping you from your bingo game."

Once he was gone, I closed my eyes and quietly murmured a lifting spell that I hoped would take care of this mess. I tried to feel the energy around me, and channel it toward the garbage. I heard it shifting against the pavement. I focused harder. Even though I was new to magic, I'd already begun to accept that the impossible was possible.

A strange feeling made my skin prickle and my eyes snapped open. A couple pieces of garbage fell from the air back to the pavement. I saw a cloaked figure at the end of the alley. There was something familiar about the way she moved. It couldn't be her, could it? We were both frozen, our eyes locked, and I shuddered. I think I moved first, but she sprang into action at almost the same moment. I don't know what my plan was if I caught her. I hadn't really expected something like this to happen. Of all the possible scenarios Aunt Erma and I had discussed, this wasn't one of them. We didn't think she'd show up in broad daylight. She disappeared around the corner. I was just seconds behind her, but she was gone. I ran to the next corner and looked up and down the street. I tried to catch my breath as my breakfast pie flipped over in my stomach and threatened to reemerge.

The street was beginning to fill up with morning shoppers, and a few heads turned my way. I forced a smile. I didn't want anyone to guess that Brenda had just been here. It had happened so fast I almost questioned whether or not I had actually seen her. No, it was definitely her. I had to call Violet.

I scanned the street as I dialed. "Brenda was here." My voice was quiet, but urgent.

"I'm on my way." Violet hung up. I felt better knowing she'd be there soon. Violet and I had a rocky relationship. Back when I was running the pie shop alone, she'd kept coming in looking for Aunt Erma and making accusations. At the time, I'd thought she was a health inspector. I later learned she was a magic inspector, and a good person to have on your side.

I made my way back down the alley to the pie shop. I couldn't help but glance over my shoulder a few times to check if Brenda was following me. Those green eyes. They were burned into my memory, and I would be perfectly happy never seeing them again.

Aunt Erma's cries echoed into the empty alley and I ran through the open back door. She was leaning over the kitchen island, breathing hard. Her gray hair was a frizzy mess and her felt antlers were askew. A rolling pin was on the floor and a few of the pies we'd had cooling on the counter were now splattered across the kitchen.

"What happened?" I rushed over to Aunt Erma, my eyes scanning over her, looking for injuries.

"She was here. She got more." She pointed to the box of magic spices on the edge of the kitchen counter. Two more bottles were missing. My heart sank.

Brenda must have circled back when I had chased her.

How could I have let this happen? I should have stayed by the pie shop.

Now they had three bottles.

"Are you okay?" I asked. I put my hand on her shoulder, still looking to see if she'd been hurt.

"I fought her off. But not before ..." Aunt Erma looked at the spice box, still breathing hard. "I had the advantage. She couldn't use her magic in here, but she had the element of surprise on her side."

Violet rushed in, her eyes wild.

"The Magic Enforcement Officers are out looking for her." She grabbed Aunt Erma's arm and looked her over. "Are you okay?"

Aunt Erma nodded and stood up a little straighter. "I'm fine. Brenda's probably long gone by now." Violet nodded. "She came out of nowhere. I didn't expect her to come when I was right here. But she didn't hold back. She's desperate."

"It's my fault," I burst out. They both turned toward me, surprised. "I ran after her down the alley. I should have stayed." It all seemed so obvious now. "Are you sure you're okay?" I asked Aunt Erma.

"I'm fine, and absolutely none of this is your fault," she said firmly. She smoothed her hair down. "What's the next step?"

"For you, nothing," Violet said.

"But they're my spices," Aunt Erma protested.

"And as soon as we find them, you'll be the first person we call. Until then, open the pie shop, and keep your eyes peeled."

As though on cue, there was a knock on the front door of the shop.

"I should be out there looking!"

"Erma." Violet's voice was softer than I'd ever heard it. "We have our best people on it. I promise I'll let you know as soon as I hear something."

Aunt Erma hesitated, then nodded.

There was another knock on the front door, and Violet slipped out the back.

Aunt Erma and I looked at each other for a minute. I bent down, picked up the rolling pin off the floor, and put it in the sink.

We plastered smiles on our faces and opened the pie shop to a small, anxious crowd who burst in full of holiday energy.

"So sorry. Everything's fine. We just lost track of time," Aunt Erma assured everyone as we quickly worked to serve them.

I kept picturing Brenda's icy stare and tried not to visibly shudder. We couldn't let word get out about the stolen spices. The last thing we needed was widespread panic.

I looked at the crowd chatting about their holiday plans and felt envious of their ignorance. I wished I could focus on gift-giving and meal preparations and out-of-town guests instead of panicking about an impending magical disaster.

When I looked at Aunt Erma, I could see no trace of this morning's traumatic events. She was steady and calm, laughing and joking with the customers. I envied her ability to compartmentalize.

Aunt Erma had let it slip once just how dangerous it was that the Drakes had one bottle of spices. We had gone to Sal's bar one night to celebrate. We were celebrating a lot of things these days – our reunion, the fact that Aunt Erma wasn't a cat anymore, years of missed holidays and birthdays – and Aunt Erma had introduced me to a drink called a Fairy's Foot. I was a little hesitant because the name did not sound at all appealing, but it was actually quite delicious. Like drinking a chocolate milkshake. The smooth sweet flavor hid the fact that the drink packed quite a punch, and by our second glass Aunt Erma had completely lost her filter and was sharing information about her love life that would have made me blush if I hadn't already been flushed from the drink.

"Make sure you find someone with good hands," she was saying firmly. "The hands are just as important as the ..."

"No!" I clapped my hands over my ears. "Tell me something else."

She giggled. "Fine." She took a deep breath. "I'm worried."

"About what?"

"The missing spice bottle. Spice number three. Three, three, bo, bee." She paused to take a sip of her drink. "The things they can do with that magic." She shook her head.

"Like what?" I asked. My experience with the spices was

limited, but I didn't understand what would be so bad about them.

"The magic in them is so powerful because of the secret ingredient. That's why you have to be careful to use just a little bit in the pies and make sure you're focusing on the proper intention when you add them. I'll explain it more to you one day. Maybe when I'm sober-er." She clinked my glass with hers and began talking about highly inappropriate things again before I could ask her what the secret ingredient was.

Flora, Lena, and Mr. Barnes, more affectionately known as the Morning Pie Crew, rushed in the minute there was a lull. Flora's bookshop was kitty corner from the pie shop, and I sometimes wondered how much of her day was spent peering in our windows. She always seemed to have a pretty good handle on what was happening in the pie shop.

Lena's white hair was piled on top of her head in its usual bun, but her ever-smiling face was creased with worry. Flora's big brown eyes scanned us up and down as though searching for injuries. Mr. Barnes was wearing his usual matching fedora and vest. He put his hands on my and Aunt Erma's shoulders. I immediately felt some of my anxiety slip away. Mr. Barnes was a yoga teacher, and he specialized in calming magic.

"Are you okay? Are you okay? Are you okay?" Their voices filled the shop as they anxiously turned from Aunt Erma to me and back again.

"Yes, we're fine." Aunt Erma waved them away and started pulling plates out so she could serve them pie.

"How did you guys even know that Brenda was here?" I asked.

"Violet called me to ask if I'd seen anything," Flora explained, fiddling with the sparkly white flower pin on her sweater. "I didn't. I can't believe I wasn't watching."

"Sit, and we'll have our pie," Aunt Erma demanded. I could tell some of her confidence was an act by the way she aggressively cut into the pies and scooped them out onto their plates. She didn't like to be vulnerable.

I carefully took the plates from her and set them on the table.

"How's everyone doing today?" I asked, giving them each a meaningful look.

They took the hint and struck up a conversation about today's Ask Elodie, an advice column in the local paper. Today's column was about a husband who was going to miss the birth of his first child.

I was one of two people in town who knew that Henry was actually Elodie. He liked to keep that secret because he didn't want people hounding him when they didn't agree with his advice. Plus, I think the mystery made people more intrigued by the column.

Flora couldn't help herself for long though.

"Are you sure you're okay?" I heard her quietly ask Aunt Erma while Mr. Barnes and Lena argued about what constituted a good excuse for missing the birth of your child.

"We'll get the spices back and everything will be fine," Aunt Erma said.

She'd no sooner gotten the words out when Violet rushed in, her usually slicked-down hair now stuck out in a messy halo around her head.

"Come with me. It's already happening," she said urgently.

Aunt Erma jumped up and the rest of us followed suit.

"Since you all already know about Brenda and the stolen spices, you might as well make yourselves useful," Violet said, a hint of her sternness returning. She turned to Flora. "Can we use your basement?"

The bookstore had a basement? I'd been there several times, but I'd only seen stairs going up to Flora's apartment. Never a set going down.

"Of course," Flora said. We left our half-eaten slices of pie and filed out the door. I reached back in to hang the "Back in ten minutes" sign before locking up.

Like soldiers getting ready for battle, we marched across the street to Flora's. She led us to a small door in the back of the shop. Everyone but Flora had to crouch down to get through it.

We went down a dark narrow staircase to a room below. It was warm and cozy with a floor-to-ceiling bookshelf filled with old volumes. There was a quiet anxiousness in the room as Violet strode over to a computer with a large screen that sat on a deep mahogany desk. While we waited, Mr. Barnes cleaned his thick-rimmed glasses on the corner of his bright blue shirt. Lena reached over and patted down

16

a stray chunk of his white hair that was sticking straight up on his head after he'd taken his hat off.

"Sit," Violet demanded. We gathered chairs from around the room and pulled them up to the computer screen. I wasn't sure what we were about to see. I smiled at Lena, hoping for reassurance, and she flashed a quick smile back at me. Her bright blue eyes lacked their usual twinkle. Violet stuck a thumb drive in the computer, and a black and white video started playing. It was taken from a high angle, looking down at a crowd walking along the street. A cloud descended on the group. It was hard to see exactly what it was in the grainy picture, but suddenly the people were taking slow, even steps. Some of them turned so they were all heading in the same direction. I shivered a little at the sight. Then suddenly everyone stopped walking. People looked around as though confused, and the crowd dispersed.

"They must be having trouble making the effects last very long," Mr. Barnes said.

"But they're going to make progress more quickly now that they have more spices to work with," Aunt Erma said.

The video skipped ahead, and Stan's parents popped up on the screen. Even in the fuzzy footage, I could recognize them. They were walking along, stopped, and looked straight into the camera.

"That's strange," Flora said, her brown eyes narrowed. "They know the camera is there. Why don't they hide themselves better? They could have erased the footage if they really wanted to."

"I thought so too," Violet said. "The only conclusion I could come to is they wanted us to find them. That can only mean one thing. They're trying to draw you out, Erma."

All of our heads turned towards Aunt Erma. Her eyebrows were pinched together with worry, but she quickly rearranged her features into a brave face.

"If they want me, they'll get me," she said with a determined edge to her voice.

Chapter 2

Dear Elodie,

Last week my cousin and her two young daughters were over at my house. I fed them a meal and snacks and drinks and made sure they had games to play with. When they left, I found my favorite porcelain duck statue in pieces and stuffed behind the sofa cushion. I called my cousin to confront her about it, and she denies that her daughters did anything wrong. No one else has been at my house lately. I'm blown away. I wasn't looking for any monetary reimbursement, but I did expect an apology. I'm so mad right now, I don't ever want them in my house again. How do I get past my anger if they won't apologize?

Sincerely,
Decapitated Duck

Dear Decapitated Duck,

One word in your letter stuck out to me – confront. You called your cousin to confront her? Were you aggressive right off the bat? Sometimes when people feel attacked they respond with hostility. Yes, they should have admitted their wrongdoing, but maybe you should also re-examine how you handled their mistakes. Work toward forgiveness because your anger is hurting you more than anyone else.

Ask and I'll Answer,

Elodie

The room erupted as everyone protested at once.

"I'm going with her," I yelled over the noise.

"Neither of you is going anywhere until we figure out if this is a trap or not." Flora pulled out her stern librarian voice that made me shrink back a little.

"I have to go," Aunt Erma said, almost matching Flora's firm tone. "I'm best suited for the job since it's my magic they're altering. You know how dangerous it could be if they're successful. For everyone."

"We've been looking for them for months," Violet added. "Now we've seen them twice in one day? They must be gearing up for something."

Everyone was silent for a minute.

"Susie, I'm not sure you should go, though," Lena said. "I think I should go along with Erma."

I bristled a little at her slightly condescending tone. I might be new to this magic thing, but I knew I could be helpful. I had taken karate for three years when I was in elementary school, and kickboxing for four years in college.

There were some problems magic couldn't solve and I was ready to face them.

"We should all go," Mr. Barnes chimed in.

"That might draw too much attention," Violet said.

"Susie will come with me," Aunt Erma said firmly. "We'll go and see what's happening and report back." Everyone nodded. I noticed that when Aunt Erma talked, people tended to agree with her.

"And I'll keep an eye on you through the security cameras," Violet said, pointing at the computer screen. She had paused the image on Dennis and Brenda, and I glared at them, trying to build up my confidence. If I could keep myself from being afraid of their image, then I could definitely take them on in person. I tried not to think about Brenda's eyes.

"I'm going to need a little time to get ready," Aunt Erma said. I saw calculating curiosity in Violet's eyes.

"Fine," she said with one curt nod. "But hurry."

We emerged from the basement and headed our separate ways. Something about the way Flora hugged me before I left made my stomach clench. How dangerous was this going to be?

"Come with me." Aunt Erma grabbed my hand and led me to her car.

"Are we going now?" I asked, unable to keep the panic out of my voice.

"No," she said. "There's something I want to show you." I got in the car.

"Hold on, I'll be right back." Aunt Erma ran to the pie

shop. She only seemed to have one speed: fast. A minute later she appeared with her dog, Mitzy, close at her heels. Mitzy was a brown ball of fluff with boundless energy. Her large, expressive brown eyes reacted when you talked to her, showing a level of understanding that I often found unsettling.

Aunt Erma opened the back door and Mitzy hopped in. Her tail was wagging so hard I thought she might take flight.

"Mitzy loves a good car ride," Aunt Erma explained. The dog heard her name and somehow took it as an invitation to leap from the back seat into my lap.

"Hi, Mitzy," I said flatly. I loved Mitzy, really, but I was still getting used to this furry licking creature who lived life as if she did a shot of espresso every hour.

Aunt Erma drove through Hocus Hills, which currently looked as though Father Christmas had thrown up on every street corner. Lights twinkled on every tree and bush and along the front of every shop. I didn't see a single door without a wreath and a very elaborate winter wonderland had been set up in the town square complete with nine reindeer, several elves, and Christmas fairies. There were also banners all over town advertising the upcoming snowman-building contest. "Erma's Pies" was one of the sponsors, and Aunt Erma had been making me practice my snowman-building skills for the last two weeks.

We drove out of town and hit the highway.

"Where are we going?" I asked. The old, light blue car was finally warm, and I sank back into the brown velvet seats. Mitzy had settled down in my lap. Her previous excitement seemed to be wearing off.

"You'll see," Aunt Erma said. She turned up the volume on the radio and Christmas songs filled the car. She sang "Rudolph the Red-Nosed Reindeer" at the top of her lungs. I'd learned how to sing from her – off key, but enthusiastic. Her energy was infectious and soon I was singing too. Mitzy groaned disapprovingly and moved to the back seat of the car. I would have to remember to sing loudly next time she was bugging me.

We exited the highway and turned down a narrow, wooded road. The dark green pine trees contrasted beautifully with the white snow and silver bark of the birch trees. The trees got thicker and we turned down an even more narrow dirt road. The tires crunched against the gravel and I bit my tongue, trying to resist the urge to ask where we were going again. Finally Aunt Erma pulled over as far as she could, which wasn't far on this skinny stretch, and put the car in park.

"Is this it?" I asked, looking around expecting to see something more than trees and snow.

"Yes. Follow me." She got out of the car, and Mitzy flew over the seat to follow her. I opened the door and wrapped my red coat tighter around my body. I shivered against the cold air.

"Are you going to tell me what we're doing yet?" I hurried to keep up with her. She was half a foot shorter than I was and twice my age, but she walked so fast! I was sure her speed was the result of some sort of magic, but when I'd once asked her she'd winked and said, "It's not magic. It's yoga."

I really had to start going to more of Mr. Barnes's yoga classes this winter. Or I was going to have to stop walking with Aunt Erma.

Mitzy was frolicking in the snow but still managed to keep up. I hopped over sticks and tried to step exactly in Aunt Erma's footprints, so the deep snow didn't go over the edge of my short boots. We didn't seem to be following any path, and I couldn't imagine a building would pop up in these deserted woods. Where in the world could she be taking me? Aunt Erma stopped so abruptly and I was hurrying so fast behind her that I ran into her, unable to stop my momentum.

"Sorry," I said, scratching my nose, which had bumped against her tall fuzzy white hat.

"We're here," she said with a satisfied nod.

"We're in the middle of the woods," I said, glancing around, wondering which of us was going nutty.

"There." She pointed ahead of us.

I squinted and saw a small tree, just a few feet taller than me. It had green, red, and silver baubles hanging from the branches. Even in the dead of winter, it still had all its leaves. The leaves were thick and waxy and almost looked fake, and the light brown bark seemed to shimmer in the sunlight. The winding branches danced in the breeze and the baubles tinkled together.

"What is it?" I asked, hoping she wouldn't just answer with the obvious: "A tree."

"It's a magic tree," she said, providing an ever so slightly better explanation than I was hoping for.

"I don't understand," I said. "What's a magic tree, and why does it have ornaments on it?"

"I decorated it for Christmas," she said with a sheepish shrug of her shoulders. I nodded. That was a very Aunt Erma thing to do. She carefully touched one of the leaves, and the branches began to rustle a little harder, which was strange, as the wind hadn't picked up.

"You've probably heard a few murmurings around town about how powerful my spices are," she began slowly.

"I've heard a thing or two," I answered. That was definitely an understatement. Aunt Erma's magic was one of the most talked about "secrets" around town.

"I've always been pretty powerful," she said. She wasn't bragging, just stating a fact. "However, I found a way to be even more powerful." She gestured to the tree with a flourish of her arm. "It came to me in a dream one night. After I saw it, I woke up, got in my car, and somehow, I just knew where to go. I ended up here. This tree contains more magic than I ever even knew existed. You can feel it."

She grabbed my hand and put it on the trunk of the tree. I felt the tingling of power course through my body.

"How does it work?" I asked. I held my hand there even after she took hers away.

25

"For some of the spices, I scrape off a little of the bark, and for others, I use the leaves," she said. "It's tricky with this much power to get the intention just right. That's why I keep it simple. You know, promoting feelings of love and happiness. I never do anything big or complicated like the Drakes are trying to do. When magic goes wrong it can get really ugly." She shuddered a little.

"What do you mean?" I asked. I wanted specifics. I was tired of all of this "things can go bad with magic" stuff. I needed answers now.

"Okay, I'll tell you a story." She thought for a minute. "A while back there was an elf who was running a factory. Well, he was part elf, like we're part fairy," she added. "If he was full elf he would look like an elf – pointy ears, the whole bit."

I nodded. I began to worry that this was going to be a long-winded story, and it was cold outside. I looked around for Mitzy. She was still frolicking around the trees. Maybe it was because she was enjoying it. Or maybe she was just trying to stay warm.

"His factory made clothing," Aunt Erma continued, "and soon greed got the best of him. There are some magical people out there who believe we should be using our magic to exert power over others. He used magic to produce more and more clothing by making his workers move faster and faster until they were collapsing. Then, to make matters worse, the clothes started acting up."

"The clothes acted up?" I asked, incredulously.

"Yes, sweaters were opening and closing closet doors, socks were banging against the side of dressers. It was a disaster. People everywhere were panicking. There was a huge rush on exorcisms." Aunt Erma shook her head. "The Magic Enforcement Team was busy for months un-enchanting all of the affected clothing and altering people's memories, so they thought it was all just a strange dream."

We filled our pockets with some leaves and a couple twigs from the magic tree.

"Why don't you bring a bunch back with us?" I asked. "The more magic we have, the better, right?"

"It doesn't quite work that way." She carefully plucked one more leaf and held it up to me. "These parts of the tree slowly begin to lose magic once they've been harvested. If we harvest too much, they'll just be tree bits by the time we get around to using them." She carefully tucked the leaf in her pocket next to the others. "Plus it would be dangerous to have too much magic at the pie shop." She looked up at the tree. "It's already dangerous with what we have."

"Can we go back to the car now?" I was jumping up and down trying to keep my blood from freezing in my veins. I looked down. My feet were still there, but I could no longer feel them. I was trying to process what Aunt Erma told me, but I was pretty sure I'd need to be warm before it would really make sense.

"Yes, yes, let's go back to the car," she said, scooting back through the trees. Mitzy eagerly followed us.

"Why did you bring me here?" I asked, a little breathless as I struggled to keep up again.

"I wanted you to know where this was. In case anything happens to me," she said, matter-of-factly.

I stopped in my tracks. She was about a hundred feet ahead of me before she realized I wasn't following anymore. She turned back. I started walking again, and she waited for me.

"Is it really that dangerous?" I asked, trying to keep the quiver out of my voice.

"We'll be fine," she said firmly. "Plus, we have a vicious guard dog on our side." Mitzy yipped in agreement. I tried to smile, but I couldn't shake the anxious feeling threatening to suffocate me.

Chapter 3

Dear Elodie,

I think my roommate is trying to control my mind. I catch him staring at me sometimes intensely for long periods of time. When I ask him what he's doing, he ignores me and continues to stare. Usually I leave the room. Sometimes I even leave the apartment. The strangest part is after I catch him staring at me, I often have the urge to do his laundry or wash his dishes. That has to be coming from him, right? How do I stop him?

Sincerely,

Mind Meld Man

Dear Mind Meld Man,

It sounds like you and your roommate should spend some time apart. Maybe far apart, like in different apartments. Otherwise I'd recommend wearing a tinfoil hat and hoping for the best.

Ask and I'll Answer,

Elodie

"I'm coming with you." I could hear Lena's voice loud and clear even though Aunt Erma's cell phone was pressed to her ear.

"Now, Lena," Aunt Erma began in a tone I knew meant she was about to try and talk her out of it.

"I said I'm coming," she roared. "So help me, Erma, if you don't get back here right now ..."

"All right, we're on our way," Aunt Erma relented.

My head was spinning during the drive back to town. My thoughts had begun to blur as the car had warmed up, but there was still a swirling feeling in my stomach. Mitzy settled in my lap and as the snow melted off her fur and soaked through my pants my eyes snapped open. "Does the Morning Pie Crew know about the tree?" I asked.

She shook her head and merged onto the highway.

"You're the only one I've told."

"Why?"

"It's safer. People can get strange around that much power. Even the most trustworthy people ..." Her voice trailed off, and she tightened her grip on the steering wheel.

"I thought you guys shared everything." I couldn't help but feel a little proud to be in on the secret, but it scared me too.

"Everyone has secrets," she said. She pressed her lips together and kept her eyes fixed to the road.

I stopped prying. I stared at the road too until we returned to Hocus Hills.

Lena was waiting on the curb in front of her hardware store.

"I'm driving," she announced once Erma had pulled up and rolled down the window. "We'll get there faster." She turned on her heel before Aunt Erma could protest. Aunt Erma rolled her eyes and parked the car.

"I'll be right back. I have to put Mitzy in the apartment," she said. I saw her sneak around to the alley with Mitzy in tow. There were a few people peering in the windows of the pie shop. I remembered the "Back in ten minutes" sign with a twinge of guilt. They'd probably forgive me if only they knew we were going to save the world from the power-hungry Drake family. Unfortunately I wouldn't be able to give them that excuse.

Minutes later I was in the back seat of Lena's car, clinging to the handle by the window with one hand and gripping the plush blue seat with the other. Speed limits were merely a suggestion in Lena's world. I swear as we rounded the corners, the car tipped up on two wheels. When I said this out loud, Lena told me to stop being so dramatic.

"You'll thank me when we get there and get this taken care of quickly," she said, speeding up as the light in front of us changed from green to yellow.

"Here, eat this." Aunt Erma handed small squares to me and Lena before popping one into her own mouth.

"What is it?" I asked.

"It will protect you," Aunt Erma answered.

"From what, a car accident?" I asked.

"The magic."

I inspected the square before eating it. It was white with little green flecks in it. Was it part of the tree? I glanced at Aunt Erma and she gave me a sharp look, confirming my suspicion. I took a tentative bite. It tasted like salt-water taffy, so I put the rest in my mouth and chewed. I always expected to hear wind chimes when I ate something magical, but to this date that had not happened.

In between muttering wishes for a safe arrival, I asked about the plan.

"What happens if we find the Drakes?"

"We play a game of shake the Drakes," Lena said in such a deep, sinister voice that despite my nerves I couldn't help but laugh.

"If we see the Drakes, you, Susie, will call Violet," Aunt Erma began. "And you, Lena, will detain Stan and Dennis. I will take care of Brenda."

Why did I always end up with the lamest jobs? While others would go down in history books for saving the world and taking down the bad guys, I would be credited in the footnotes for making a phone call.

We squealed into a parking spot on the street at the edge of town.

"We should walk in so we can sneak up on what's happening. Get a feel for what we're getting into," Aunt Erma suggested.

"Everyone take note of where we parked in case we get separated." Lena pointed to the street signs on the corner.

My stomach flipped. In case we got separated? That thought hadn't even crossed my mind. I began to regret my insistence to come along. I glanced at Aunt Erma, and she reached over and squeezed my arm. For a moment I felt as if everything was going to be okay.

I was on high alert. My ears strained to hear something that sounded like evil magic. It was quiet except for the wind that whistled around the buildings. A paper bag blew by like a tumbleweed. By this time of day, the streets should have been bustling. It felt like a scene from a horror movie but even more surreal. I scanned the windows of every building we passed and braced myself in case Brenda's face appeared. We peeked into a bakery. It should have been full of people buying their bread and doughnuts, but it was empty.

I positioned myself in the middle as we walked shoulder to shoulder towards the center of town and resisted the urge to reach out and grab Aunt Erma's hand for protection.

"Where is everyone?" I whispered. The layout of the town was similar to Hocus Hills except their town square was a little smaller, and there was a duck pond near the gazebo.

Lena shrugged.

"I don't know, but it can't be good," Aunt Erma said.

I stopped in my tracks. "I hear something," I said. They both stopped, and I held my breath as we listened. There was a sound coming from the church.

"We need more yarn," we heard a deep voice yell. The church was a large white wooden building with steps leading up to a set of dark wood double doors. We crept up the steps, and Lena pushed the door open a crack. She peeked inside.

"I think we found everyone," she said, pushing the door the rest of the way open.

The church was jam-packed with people of all ages. It was a flurry of activity, but I couldn't figure out what they were doing. Some people were rushing around the room picking up skeins of yarn and moving them from one pew to another. Several people were knitting. Knitting? This seemed like more than just a quirky small-town activity. There was a large red circle that looked like a knitted parachute. People were working on different edges.

"What are they making?" Lena wondered aloud.

"A mitten," a man with an armload of yarn balls yelled as he rushed past us.

"The world's largest," one of the women who was knitting called.

"Are the Drakes here?" The room was packed, but I didn't see any sign of them.

Aunt Erma shook her head. "I don't feel their magic. It's strange that they're not here though." She looked a little uneasy, and I took a small step closer to her.

"Why is everyone knitting?" I asked. I almost felt dizzy from the hysteria around us.

"It must be part of the spell," Aunt Erma said.

"But why?" I asked. It seemed like such a strange activity, and not at all in line with their ultimate goal of more power.

"It's probably an accident," Aunt Erma said. "They're too power hungry to focus on getting the spell right. They're frenzied as they alter the spices. It's very hard to get the intention right – takes a lot of finesse. That's why you should always keep it simple." She was speaking to me now. I wasn't sure it was the time for a magic lesson, but I nodded as I looked around at the chaos. I certainly didn't ever want this to happen.

"How are we going to break the spell?" Lena asked, jumping out of the way of a frantic boy who was chasing the yarn balls he had just dropped as they rolled across the floor.

"Do we need to break it?" I asked, looking around. I mean, what they were doing was crazy, but it didn't seem to be harmful. Unless they started capturing people inside the giant mitten once they finished knitting it.

"It could be dangerous to leave them like this. They won't be able to stop until they've finished no matter how tired they are, and some of them could actually work themselves to death," Aunt Erma said. Okay, that sounded bad. She was surveying the scene intently. "Lena, do you have them?"

"I told you you'd need me," she said as she fished around in her yellow purse. She set it on the floor, and her whole head disappeared as she leaned into it. I was tempted to grab her feet, so she wouldn't fall in. I didn't know what exactly was inside there. I had asked her once how the magic purse worked. Was it just like a closet or was there a whole house inside?

"Oh no, dear, I couldn't tell you that. Your aunt may be ready to divulge all of her secrets, but I like to keep one or two up my sleeve," she had said.

"Ah, yes, here it is." Her muffled voice emerged from the purse a second before she did. She triumphantly held up a stack of Erma's Pies boxes.

"You keep pie in there?" I asked.

"You never know when you'll need some," she said. "Impromptu dinner party, afternoon snack, an antidote to stop crazed knitters."

Aunt Erma took the boxes from Lena and opened the lid. She took a deep breath.

"The triple berry. Yes, this one should work. The unaltered spices will counteract the altered spices they used." She pulled a bottle out of her pocket. It was clear and plain, not like her other spice bottles, but it had green flakes in it. I recognized them as leaves from the tree but I didn't know when she'd had a chance to crumble them up and put them in a bottle. She sprinkled a healthy dose on top of all the pies. "A little extra boost," she explained.

"They're not all going to eat willingly. We're going to have to coax them," Lena said.

Lena did some more digging in her purse and emerged with three forks and a knife. We each took a pie. I watched

Aunt Erma approach a young man who was knitting and offer him a bite of pie. He shook his head vehemently, his sandy brown hair flopping across his face. Without missing a beat, Aunt Erma shoved a bite into his mouth. His eyes widened so much I thought they might pop out of his head. He chewed and swallowed, all the while making "Mmmm" noises. Then his face changed. His brow furrowed, and he looked around.

"What's going on?" he asked.

"Don't worry about it," Lena said. "You're just having a strange dream. Go home."

The man shrugged and shuffled off.

"All right, everyone, understand the plan?" Aunt Erma asked.

Lena and I nodded. Then we all set off, shoving small bites of pie into people's mouths as we went. Some of the people I encountered eagerly opened their mouths when offered pie – they were probably hungry after all this knitting – while others proved to be a bit more challenging. I dodged a man who tried to jab me with a knitting needle. I snuck behind him and reached around to shove a forkful of pie into his mouth.

"Aren't they all going to talk and figure out they had the same strange dream?" I asked Lena as I airplaned a bite into a young girl's mouth. Lena did the same with the girl's mother. The girl dropped the yarn ball she had been winding up and followed her mother out the door.

"Most of them will have forgotten about this completely

by tomorrow. Only a few will have a distant memory of this strange dream," she said. "It won't be enough for them to put it together that it actually happened."

"Some of them might be a little sore tomorrow from all the work," Aunt Erma said as she ran past, chasing a man with gray hair and thick glasses. The man threw a ball of yarn at Aunt Erma, and she tackled him and shoved the bite of pie into his mouth before he could stop her.

I was bitten at least six times, but we finally cleared the church of all frantic knitters. I leaned against the wall and began planning which pajamas I was going to put on as soon as I got home – the footy pajamas with the turtle print – and what I was going to eat – pizza with three sides of pie.

"We have to get all this out of here." Aunt Erma motioned to the giant knitted circle that had yet to take shape as the largest mitten in the world.

"Why?" I asked. I didn't want to let anything keep me from that pizza any longer than necessary.

"It's a lot harder to convince people it was a dream when they can come to the church and find two tons of yarn and a knitted circle as large as a parachute.

After we'd cleared everything, dispersing some of it to different shops and shoving the rest of it into the back of Lena's car, we headed back to Hocus Hills.

"What are those?" I asked as we pulled into town, pointing at a light pole plastered with sheets of paper.

"I'm not sure." Lena slowed the car down. Aunt Erma finished reading first and gasped.

In big bold letters, the signs said, "Tired of hiding? It's time to work for the Improvement for Magical People. If you're ready to step out of the shadows, stay tuned for more information from the IMPs." The flyers were everywhere.

"It was all a circus. They just wanted to get you out of town, so you couldn't stop them from doing this," Lena practically yelled.

Aunt Erma let her head fall to the back of the seat. "I don't know why we didn't see that before." She sighed.

A crew led by Violet was already pulling posters down.

"We were so focused on what you guys were doing that we didn't even see this happen until it was too late," she said. "They worked fast. It was done in a matter of seconds."

Aunt Erma's brow furrowed. "Their magic is getting stronger."

"I know. The regular spells aren't working to clean it up, so we're doing it the non-magic way," Violet said.

I grabbed a bag and went to work, quickly pulling signs off the light poles and the sides of buildings.

"Hey." Holly appeared by my side. "I hear you saved the world from crazed knitters."

"Yup, I'm a regular superhero," I said. "What's their deal anyway?" I held up the signs I'd just yanked off the front of the florist shop.

"There are some people who think that non-magical

people should be hiding from us since we're supposedly the more powerful ones," she said. "Personally, I think they should just chill. Our life here is pretty great, and it could be really dangerous for magic to get out in the world."

"How long have they been around?"

"I don't know. A long time, but they haven't really been active for the last several years. Everyone thought they disbanded and gave up. No one realized Alice was part of this bigger movement until the posters were plastered everywhere," she said.

"How do we stop them?"

"We keep them from getting too much magic."

It sounded so easy and so impossible at the same time. They had some of Aunt Erma's spices, but they didn't know about the tree. I saw a small group of people by the gazebo looking at one of the fliers and talking animatedly. I inched closer, pretending to be focused on my job of cleaning up.

"I was trying to do a spell to fix my roof last year, and the Magic Enforcers stopped me because the magic was too big." The sarcasm was clear in his voice.

"It's Violet. She's out there squashing magic. Maybe if she'd let people practice more, we wouldn't have people attacking our town and our neighbors. We'd be equipped to fight them off," a woman said.

"The IMPs might bring a breath of fresh air. We've been stuck living like this for so long, we don't even consider new ideas anymore," another woman chimed in.

I quickly scooted away, stuffing another handful of fliers

into my almost full bag. I had to go tell Aunt Erma what I'd heard.

I found her heading back toward the pie shop. A crowd had gathered outside, and people began to stir when they saw Aunt Erma approaching. I grabbed her and quickly told her what I'd overheard.

"How are we going to deal with this?" I asked.

"I'll tell Violet." Her forehead wrinkled. "This is exactly what they want."

"The IMPs?" I asked.

She nodded. The clean-up was almost done so I headed to the pie shop to help.

"Come in, everyone," she said as she shuffled between the grumbling crowd to unlock the front door. "Thanks for your patience. Coffee for everyone, on the house!"

"Someone was looking for you," Nadine, one of our regulars, whose blonde curly hair was always gathered in a poof on top of her head, said to me. As far as I could tell, her job in town was to spread gossip.

"Oh yeah? Who?" I asked, following her through the door.

"I don't know. Some guy."

"Henry?" I asked, even though I figured he would call me if he was looking for me.

"No, some curly-haired guy I haven't seen before." She shrugged.

"I guess this mystery man will have to come back if he wants to talk to me." I went back to the kitchen and stopped in my tracks.

"Mom," I said.

"You recognize me. I'm so touched," she said, barely looking up as she sliced a peppermint cream pie. My mom's brown hair was just a shade lighter than mine. Unlike mine, it was smooth and perfectly styled. Instead of her usual business suit, she wore jeans and a dark green sweater.

My mother had gone back to the city a couple weeks after Aunt Erma had become human again after being a cat. We'd had a wonderful week where our days were full of baking and gossiping – we were a regular holiday special! – then the bickering had begun, and the comments under our breath, and my mother had decided she had to get back to her clients at home. I didn't blame her. It was a lot of intense family time after a long separation.

"She'll be back soon," Aunt Erma had reassured me as I had watched her car drive away with a lump in my throat. I had been enjoying the gossiping and reminiscing. It had been so long since I'd seen my mother laugh that much.

That was less than two weeks ago, and here she was again. I guess I didn't have anything to worry about.

"Erma called and asked me to come help at the pie shop while you guys went on some sort of mission." My mother began cutting the next pie more forcefully than was actually necessary.

"We have to go—" I began.

"No," my mother cut me off, still keeping her eyes on the pie. "I don't want to know. I know it has to be dangerous. I could tell from Erma's tone. It's best if I just worry here instead of knowing the specifics. I'll just serve pie and worry."

Ah, my mother the martyr.

"How long are you here for?" I asked.

"I booked a room at the inn for three nights, but we'll see," she answered. My mother preferred to stay at the local inn instead of squishing into the apartment with us.

Aunt Erma had already fulfilled the orders of the crowd before sneaking to the back of the kitchen to make a phone call. She faced the corner and spoke in a low voice, probably talking to Violet. The angry grumbles out front had turned into happy chattering as people drank their free cups of coffee.

"I'm taking my cats to see Santa," someone said.

"My sister is coming to visit with her four children, and they're all staying in my one-bedroom apartment," I heard someone else say as I filled an empty mug with more steaming coffee.

"My husband is in a Christmas play, and he wants me to go watch all twelve performances," another voice chimed in.

I heard a familiar voice say my name. I saw him in the crowd, but it didn't register because he was a familiar face in an unfamiliar place. I was shocked and speechless for a moment.

"Josh," I finally managed to croak, reaching out to hug him.

"Hey, Susie." He was warm and smelled like sawdust. He held me for a second longer after I had let go.

"What are you doing here?" I asked, taking a step back to look at him. His dark curly hair had gotten a little long. He had dark circles under his brown eyes, and his usually rosy cheeks were pale. "Is everything okay?"

"Hal has me working at a big remodel in Mavisville," he said. Mavisville was another nearby town. "It should take a couple of weeks."

"That's great. We'll definitely have to get together to catch up," I said.

"Someone gave me one of these." He held up one of the IMP fliers, and I snatched it out of his hand.

"That's for a holiday play the town is putting on. They're very creative here." I could hear my voice coming out a little too high-pitched as I crumpled the paper and stuffed it into my pocket.

"I need to talk to you," he said.

At least four people in the store stopped their conversations to openly stare at us.

"Let's go outside." I grabbed the sleeve of his coat and led him towards the front door.

"Who is that?" I heard someone whisper loudly as I opened the door.

"Beats me. I'd bet an old boyfriend," someone else said.

I glared over my shoulder in the general direction of the voices. Josh and I had been co-workers back home. We had grown to be good friends, but it was never anything more than that. Josh was the one I'd call when I was having trouble with a relationship, and I would give him insights on the people he dated whether he asked for it or not. I hadn't really talked to him since I'd left – just a couple quick text messages that didn't really say much.

I wrapped my gray sweater more tightly around myself and faced him. I thought longingly of my red coat hanging on the hook at the back of the kitchen. Why had I suggested going outside? The mid-December wind was biting against my skin. Oh yeah, outside was the only place we had a shot at not being eavesdropped on. However, if anyone could lip-read, we were in trouble as all of the customers in the shop were blatantly staring through the window. They practically had their noses pressed against the glass.

I took a couple of steps back toward the flower shop next door so we were at least a little out of sight, though I wasn't sure there was anywhere completely out of sight in this town ...

Josh stared at the ground for a minute.

"Is everything okay?" I asked again. I wanted this to hurry up, so I could get back to the toasty warm kitchen.

"So, you live here now?" he asked, looking up and down the street.

"I think so," I said with a shrug. "I haven't really figured it out long term yet. I live here for now, I guess."

"I'm glad you got to reunite with your aunt," he said. Josh had heard my sob story more than once about my long-lost Aunt Erma. Usually it was after a bad day at work or a fight with my mom and a few beers.

"Yeah, it's been nice," I said. It was silent for a minute, and I was about to tell him I had to go back inside.

"You didn't even say goodbye to me," he said suddenly, meeting my eyes for the first time since we'd stepped outside.

"What?"

"We were friends. Maybe more. At least I thought we were." He said the last part more to himself than to me.

I opened my mouth. Nothing but air came out.

"Was I just imagining it? I kind of thought we were on track to get together. I thought you felt it too. Heck, I've loved you since I saw you fix that hole on the side of the Morrow's house. You were fearless at the top of the ladder while the rest of us were too chicken to climb that high."

I remembered that job. I had been terrified too, but I had been new at Hal's Handyman Services, and I'd wanted to show off in front of my new co-workers. Afterwards I'd had to excuse myself to the side of the house where I'd promptly thrown up in a trash can. I thought back to my time with Josh. Had I missed the signs? Sure, we had been good friends. I would even consider him to be one of my best friends. I hadn't meant to drop him when I came to Hocus Hills, but finding my long-lost aunt, discovering magic was real, and trying to squash an evil plot to take over the world all took up a lot of one's free time.

"Josh, I ..." I paused for a minute. "I'm sorry I didn't

say goodbye." It sounded lame when I said it. He looked at me expectantly. "And I'm sorry I haven't kept in touch better. It's been so crazy around here."

I didn't even know where to begin with his other confessions. There had been a time a few years ago when I'd thought about him that way. I'd even tried to flirt with him and hang out with him more than usual, but shortly after I'd begun to have those feelings, he'd started dating a woman his sister had set him up with. It had been serious for a while, and I'd moved on too. I hadn't really let myself think about it again since then.

I jumped when I felt a hand on my shoulder. It was Lena.

"I hate to interrupt, but Violet wants to talk to you," she said with a polite nod towards Josh.

"Now?" I asked.

"I'm Lena." She stuck her hand out towards Josh.

"Nice to meet you, Lena. I'm Josh." He shook her hand. "I'm a friend of Susie's from back home."

She looked at me with raised eyebrows.

"So, we need to get going, huh?" I said.

"Right, yes," she said.

"Bye, Josh. I'll call you later." I followed Lena inside, trying to ignore the guilty feeling in the pit of my stomach when I looked over my shoulder and saw him watching me go.

The chatter inside the pie shop stopped immediately when I came through the door. No doubt they'd all been talking about me. I ignored them and went back to the kitchen where Violet was waiting. My mother moved out front to help customers, clearly not wanting any part of this conversation.

I told Violet everything I'd overheard by the gazebo and what the people looked like. She thanked me and told me to keep my ears open and let her know if I heard anything else.

After she left, I thought about what Josh had said. Henry and I were having such a wonderful time, but Josh and I went way back. He was comfortable in a way that only someone you'd known a long time could be. He was like a thick warm comforter. But with Henry there was a spark. People always said the spark didn't last forever – that you needed more in your relationship besides electricity – but the spark sure felt good right now. Maybe it would develop into the comfortable relationship I had with Josh. Maybe it would be even better. Plus, Henry knew about magic. There was a whole part of my new life that I wasn't sure if I could share with Josh. The people of Hocus Hills were very private about their magic, and I certainly didn't blame them. You never knew who you could trust, and if word got out that there were magic people in the world, there would be chaos.

The crowd at the shop was starting to clear out when Holly came in.

"I felt like I deserved pie after all my hard work doing

trash pick-up," she said, casually leaning against the display case.

"I completely agree. What can I get you?"

"I heard you had some hunky, curly-haired stranger show up today." She was carefully reading the options on the chalkboard.

"Hunky?" I asked.

"My mother's words, not mine," she said.

"How did she see him?"

"Nadine texted her a picture," she said, as though the answer were obvious.

"What?"

"I forgot you're still new to this small-town living where everyone knows your business," she said. "So, what's the story?"

"Josh is a friend from back home," I said evasively.

"Two men vying for your love, that must be tough," she said. I let my chin fall to my chest with a groan.

"I don't know what to do," I said. "I don't want to hurt anyone's feelings."

"That's your problem," she said. "You have to stop worrying about their feelings and think about what you want."

"I want to learn how to windsurf," I said, thoughtfully tapping my chin.

"Fair enough," she said, and selected a piece of berry cream.

I quickly asked her about the latest book she was writing,

and she was off telling me how she wasn't sure if she should kill off one of her favorite characters or not. I was off the hook for now, but as she finished her pie we made plans for a girls' night out on Friday, and I knew there would be more questions then.

Later that night I was bundled up in my very large new red knitted blanket watching television when Henry stopped by. I struggled to get out of the cocoon I had wrapped myself in.

"Did everything go okay?" he asked after greeting me with a long hug. I studied my reaction to his hug. Had anything changed after Josh's confession? I still felt the sizzle in all the right places, I decided as I pulled away.

"I didn't realize magic was such hard work, but, yes, it went fine," I said. I was too tired to give him the details, and I was pretty sure he would have heard them already from someone in town. News spread fast. Especially the news that you wanted to keep quiet. Just yesterday I heard Mrs. Lansbury yell across the street asking Mr. Knight about his colonoscopy.

"Anything interesting happen after you saved the world?" Henry's tone was strange, as if he was trying to stay super casual, but his voice was too high and too tight.

"Oh yeah," I said, also trying to keep my tone light as though I were just remembering something that I'd actually been thinking about all day. "A friend of mine from back home stopped by."

"Really?" He tried to sound surprised, but his acting wasn't that good.

"Yeah, we were co-workers. He came to say hi." I shrugged in what I hoped was a casual gesture.

"That's an awful long way to come to say hi," he said.

"He's working on a job in Mavisville for a couple of weeks," I said.

Just then Aunt Erma bustled in. "I'm so sorry to interrupt. Henry, how are you?"

Aunt Erma's arrival saved me from an awkward conversation and her glance out of the corner of her eye told me she knew exactly what she was doing. Thank goodness for Aunt Erma.

Henry left after a little more small talk, saying he had some work to finish, which I knew meant his "Ask Elodie" advice column. I had asked him once if all the letters were sent in from people in town. He'd said some of them were, but on the days there weren't any letters he would make them up and then answer them as Elodie. "So, you set up a problem you know you can answer?" I had teased him.

Then I'd begun to quiz him about which ones he had written. "I'm not going to ruin the magic for you by giving away all the secrets," he'd said.

I felt bad for not telling him more about Josh, but I wanted to be able to process it more myself first. I hadn't figured out how to present the facts because I hadn't figured out how I felt about the whole thing.

The truth would come out eventually though.

Chapter 4

Dear Elodie,

My sister recently moved back to town. She had lived out of state for the last fifteen years. I'm so excited about her return and want to invite her along to everything I do. My problem is the only thing she wants to do is square dance. She turns down all of my invitations and will only call me once a week to ask me to go square dancing with her. I'll be honest, I hate square dancing, but I'll go to be with my sister. I've tried telling her I would like her to come along to some of the things I invite her to, but she just dismisses me, saying she's busy. Am I wrong to be upset by this? Can I quit square dancing without quitting my sister?

Sincerely,
Round Peg in a Square Dancing Hole

Dear Round Peg in a Square Dancing Hole,

It sounds like you've given your sister every opportunity to do something other than square dance with you,

53

and you've made your feelings known. It's possible she feels overwhelmed. If she's been away from family for fifteen years, it could take some adjusting before she's used to your invitations. Maybe she's getting just as many invitations from other family members. Also, if you keep doing exactly what she wants, she has no reason to accept your invitations. Maybe you can square dance with her one week and the next week you can tell her you're busy on square dancing night, but if she'd like to go to dinner with you a different night, that would be wonderful.

    Ask and I'll Answer,

Elodie

The next morning, I woke up to the smell of pancakes. I took a deep breath and stretched out on the sofa. Mitzy, so excited to see movement, catapulted onto my face.

I yelped, thinking for the umpteenth time that I needed to get my own place. I had been looking. Sort of. But part of me wasn't sure it was worth the effort. Was this just a temporary move or a more permanent one? Life in Hocus Hills had been so crazy from the moment I got here that I hadn't thought about my life in the city much since I'd arrived. Josh's arrival reminded me of the simple comforts I had there – an apartment to myself, a job I was good at, and weeks on end without the threat of being attacked by some power-hungry magical person.

"Oh good, you're up," Aunt Erma said, peeking her head around the corner from the kitchen.

"Yup, thanks to the fuzzy alarm clock here." I pointed to Mitzy, who danced around on the floor next to me. She was like that friend that everyone had. The one that thought you were best friends even though you weren't. She never sensed my hesitation to reciprocate her affections.

"I made chocolate-chip pancakes," she said, holding up a steaming plate.

"Yum." I was off the sofa now. I poured myself a cup of coffee. "What's on the agenda for today? Please tell me we're not tackling a town who's set on making the world's largest pot-holder, are we? I'm still recovering from yesterday."

"No, nothing like that," Aunt Erma said. "At least, not that I know of," she added.

"Look at this." I pulled up the side of my shirt to show her two small bruises on my ribs. "Someone jabbed me with their knitting needles. I guess I should consider myself lucky that they didn't skewer me."

Aunt Erma inspected the bruises closely, her brow furrowed. She ran her finger over them, and I flinched.

"That's not good," she said. "They shouldn't be able to hurt you."

"What do you mean? Was I supposed to have some sort of magical shield around me? Because I definitely forgot to wear my armor yesterday." I scooped a couple of pancakes onto my plate and slathered them with butter. "Do you think they make such a thing? Like giant thimbles for your body."

"They shouldn't have been able to hurt you because none of the magic from my spices should make people do that," she said.

"But the Drakes changed them. Can't they make the magic do whatever they want?"

She shook her head firmly. "Not *my* magic. Not like this."

I stared at her, waiting for more of an explanation.

"I'm careful. Even if they redirect the power, they shouldn't be able to redirect my original intention," she said.

I nodded slowly, not sure I completely understood. "But aren't some people inclined to hurt other people? Maybe it was the person, not the magic."

"Yeah, maybe," Aunt Erma said, but I could tell she was still concerned.

"Have you heard anything more from Violet?" I asked.

She shook her head. "And today we're not going to think about it."

"We're not?" I asked, my mouth full of chocolate-chip pancakes. I knew if my mother was here, she would remind me that she raised me better than to talk with my mouth full, but the pancakes were just so darn good. They were light and fluffy, and the chocolate chips were melted just right. Aunt Erma had even topped them with whipped cream and shaped them like animals as she used to do when I was a kid. I was eating the ear off a dog when I noticed Mitzy giving me a disapproving glare.

"How does she know I'm eating the dog pancake?" I wondered under my breath.

"Magic," Aunt Erma said with a wink. "Now today, instead of focusing on the evil plot to take over our beloved town, we are going to decorate for Christmas."

"Decorate? Even more than we already have?" I asked. I thought about all the tinsel we'd hung and the cardboard Santa cutouts in every corner of the shop downstairs.

"Yes, we're just getting started," she said, sitting down across from me with her own stack of pancakes and a cup of coffee. "We have paper snowflakes to make for the snowman-building competition. Last year I cut out three hundred tiny snowflakes and hung them all over the square. It was beautiful, if I do say so myself. I used this glittery paper that was thin, slippery, and a little hard to work with, but it was worth it."

I tried not to cringe at the thought of cutting out paper snowflakes. It sounded like just the kind of project I would normally try to find an excuse to escape.

"Don't you need me to run the pie shop? We've been pretty busy lately," I said. I felt proud of my valid excuse to avoid this task.

"Don't worry, your mother is coming, and we can all take turns serving people as they come in. The Morning Pie Crew is coming too. Flora has a project she thought we'd all enjoy as well. I think it has something to do with folding paper flowers out of book pages. I think to make

57

garlands to hang around trees." I tried to hold in a groan. "But anyway, they'll be able to help while they're here too."

"Don't they have their own shops to run?" I asked. Now I was desperate to get out of this. Mr. Barnes was a yoga teacher, so I knew he had some free time depending on his schedule, but Lena ran the hardware store, and Flora owned the bookstore. Didn't people need to fix things and buy books this time of year?

"All their holiday employees are up to speed and can do without them for a few hours. Plus, today's going to be quiet. Lots of people are getting ready for the snowman-building contest," she said. "Which reminds me, we probably need to practice a few more times."

Wow, this day just kept getting better and better.

It turned out my knitting injuries weren't a good enough excuse to get out of snowflake making. Two hours later I could barely feel my fingers. Lena, Flora, Mr. Barnes, my mother, Aunt Erma, and I all crowded around two of the three tables at the front of the pie shop. Customers were wandering in here and there, and I always made sure I was the first one to leap out of my chair to serve them. In between Aunt Erma explained the importance of the paper snow-flakes.

"We'll use them as part of a protection spell in the town square," she said.

"Isn't there some magical way to cut them out?" I asked

as I held up yet another disappointing snowflake. Aunt Erma kept assuring me that they were good.

"Every snowflake is supposed to be different, and yours sure are different," Lena said.

"Thanks," I said, glaring at her a little.

"You can't magic away everything," Aunt Erma said. "We aren't in a children's movie."

"In order for them to have power, we have to cut them out by hand," Flora explained.

I sighed and folded another piece of paper. A customer walked in and, of course, I was the first one behind the counter. I took my time serving them. So much so that they began drumming their fingers on the counter. The nerve! Hadn't they ever heard of small-town charm? Where the service was slow, but the people were friendly, and your mailman was also the barber?

"So, tell us about that fella I saw you with," Lena said during a lull in the conversation.

All eyes turned to me. There was no getting out of this now.

"Oh, you mean Josh?" I asked, buying time, trying to figure out what I was going to tell them.

My mother's eyebrows shot up. "Josh was here?" She had speculated many times that Josh had feelings for me, and I had repeatedly reassured her that she was imagining things. The smug look on her face grated on me.

"He just came to say hi. He's working on a job nearby. I didn't get much of a chance to talk to him," I said.

We must have said his name too many times and summoned him because all of a sudden he walked through the door.

"Hi, Josh," I said, trying to keep my tone calm, but it came out a little too high-pitched. The whole table's eyes went from me to him and back to me again.

He froze for a second when he saw me at a table full of people. He quickly regained his composure.

"Hi, Susie. Hi, Mrs. Daniels," he said, nodding towards my mom. "Hi, everyone else. I didn't mean to interrupt. Maybe I can come back later." He backed towards the door so quickly he almost tripped over his own feet.

"Nonsense," Lena said pulling up another chair to our already crowded table. "There's plenty of room here, and we could really use some help cutting these snowflakes. I think Erma wants to fill the entire town with them."

Aunt Erma rolled her eyes. "Oh, quit being a drama queen, Lena. I'll share some of these with you."

"I run a hardware store. I can't have people getting distracted by all these sparkly snowflakes," she grumbled, but I saw her perk up a little.

Josh sat down on the corner of the chair, his hands folded tightly in his lap. He looked about as awkward as I felt. After five minutes though, he had Mr. Barnes showing him how to do the eagle pose and had Flora glowing when they discussed their favorite books, and he and Lena got into a heated discussion over which brand of drill was the best. That was how Josh was. He was quiet, but had a way of charming everyone around him easily. I had always admired that skill. I had a way of alienating or making people uncomfortable with my failed jokes. He hadn't fully won over Aunt Erma yet though. She eyed him skeptically when he asked her about the best method for making pie crust. My mother was already in love with him, so he didn't have to bother with anything more than a little small talk with her. Sometimes I wondered if my mother would rather have him as a child than me.

I was deep in thought about how I would explain this group date to Henry when I heard Josh say, "I'd love to come. Thank you so much for the invitation."

"You'd love to come where?" I asked.

"He's going to celebrate Christmas dinner with us," Flora said.

"What?" I asked. It came out sounding a little more harsh than I intended. This was going to be my first Christmas with Henry, the last thing I needed was Josh hanging around being Josh-like or trying to find the perfect moment to proclaim his undying love to me. I had been looking forward to a day of organized chaos. Adding Josh to the mix completely messed up my plans.

Just then, Henry himself walked through the door. "Henry!" the room greeted him in chorus. I waved a crooked snowflake at him.

"You're pretty good at that." He pointed at my pile.

"Don't patronize me." I glared at him. He smiled innocently at me and I couldn't help but smile back.

61

He noticed Josh and extended his hand. "I'm Henry."

Josh stood up and shook it, introducing himself.

"Josh is my friend from back home who I told you about," I said. I saw Henry's eyes quickly size up Josh, and I could feel the gaze of the group as they studied every nuance of our reactions. I tried to keep a neutral expression, but all the muscles in my face were straining to react. React how, I wasn't sure, but I didn't want my face to reveal to the room what I was feeling before I had a chance to figure it out myself.

"I should really get going," Josh said. "Thanks for letting me join in the fun." He puffed up his chest a little as he said goodbye to Henry. I got up to follow him out because we still needed to talk, but a large group walked through the door clamoring for pie.

"Can you help, Susie?" Aunt Erma asked, likely sensing my hesitation about going after Josh. I sighed and turned back to the front counter to serve pie.

"We found the perfect patch of snow," Aunt Erma announced when she and Mitzy got back from their afternoon walk. "We'll have to go quick and double back a few times. I saw Nancy Harrington eyeing me as though she knew I'd found fresh snow."

"Great." I tried to sound enthusiastic. I was enjoying the warmth of the pie-shop kitchen and in no hurry to bury my hands in the snow and lose feeling in my feet.

"Maybe we should run to the hardware store to see if we can find something better for the eyes. The bolts we've been using give our snowman a blank stare." Aunt Erma had been against using the traditional coal for eyes because it was "too expected". She also didn't want to use the wiggle eyes because she didn't want our snowman to look like a raving lunatic. I was pretty sure we'd tried hundreds of different items in an attempt to get the perfect expression to satisfy Aunt Erma.

"Don't worry, I'll go." I grabbed my coat and was out the door before she could respond. I knew whatever I got would be wrong, but going to the hardware store with Aunt Erma was always painful. She didn't understand that the hardware store was a sacred space to be appreciated and explored and instead opted for more of a "get in get out" approach.

Lena was rearranging her display of outdoor Christmas decorations when I got there. She greeted me warmly as she moved an inflatable Santa Claus to the other side of his inflatable sleigh.

"Do you need any help?" I asked.

"Nah, I'm just playing around." She smiled and put her hands on her hips. "How's everything going for you?" She nudged the Santa over another few inches.

"I'm thinking of staying." I blurted out the words before I could stop myself.

"In Hocus Hills?" she asked.

I nodded.

"Really?" She carefully studied my face while her expression remained annoyingly neutral.

"Do you think it's a good idea?"

"I think the real question is, do *you* think it's a good idea?"

I slowly blew out a breath. "I'm not sure if it's too much too soon. Twenty years apart and then, bam, now we're together all the time."

"Erma's thrilled you're here, but you have to do what's best for yourself. That's all she wants too."

"Maybe." I turned to one of the crystal baubles hanging in the window. I wondered if I stared at it long enough if it would show me my future.

"What's keeping you from staying?"

"There's a really good pizza place around the corner from my apartment. They know the perfect mushroom to green olive ratio. Plus in the city I can go days without having anyone look deep into my eyes as though they're trying to see into my soul. Like you're doing right now!" I accused, taking a step back.

"What about Henry?"

I turned my attention back to the bauble. "I feel like I'm at one of those crossroads moments in my life. Which path do I take? Is one better than the other?" I was talking more to myself now.

"Pizza and privacy? Is that really all that's holding you back?"

"Look, magic is a lot to take in. Just a few weeks ago, spells and fairy dust were only things I'd read about as a child. Now I'm learning how to use them. That's just ... crazy. I'm not sure I'm ready to live in this reality forever."

"Does Josh have anything to do with this?"

"No!" My answer came out a little louder than I intended, and I felt my cheeks flush.

"You know, a big change now doesn't have to be a permanent change. You don't even have to make a decision today. You can stay at Erma's a while longer."

"No, I can't. Have you ever slept on that sofa?" I rubbed my lower back.

"A couple times."

"Sober?"

"No ..." She giggled to herself.

"After a few nights it feels like sleeping on this table. Then there's the furry alarm clock."

"Mitzy?"

"I've started having recurring dreams that I'm an ice-cream cone. I've woken up too many times with her tongue up my nose."

"It sounds like you could use a little space. Let me take you out to look at apartments. There's no harm in looking. Maybe knowing your options will help you make your decision." I'd heard Lena was a realtor on the side. I contemplated her offer for a moment.

"As long as we can keep it a secret. I don't want everyone weighing in before I've made up my mind."

She laughed. "There's no such thing as secrets here."

I bought a variety of nuts and bolts and brought them

back to the pie shop. Aunt Erma then led me in circles around town until she was sure no one was following us. The patch of fresh snow was in the back corner of an abandoned lot. I got to work, but my head was on apartments and my future.

"The middle isn't round enough," she said.

"It's getting cold out here," I said. "Can I try again tomorrow?"

"One more time," she said. She paced back and forth in front of me.

"Wouldn't it be weird if I win though? Since we're sponsoring?" I could hear a little whine in my voice, and I was ever so slightly embarrassed, but being this cold made me revert to my younger self.

"I can't win, but you can," she said. "Only the owners of the sponsoring businesses are disqualified. If we didn't let any of the employees win, half the town wouldn't be eligible to compete." Because that would be such a shame? I wondered. "The head is lopsided." It turned out when it came to snowman-building competitions, Aunt Erma was like the worst overbearing pageant mom out there.

"Can't we just use magic?" I asked as I carefully rounded out the middle ball.

"Magic is forbidden at these competitions," she said. "At least until after the judging, when everyone makes the snowmen dance." She giggled. "Lena made hers twerk last year. I didn't even know what twerking was until then."

66

"Yeah, Lena's pretty hip." I rubbed my hands together through the mittens before reassembling my snowman.

Aunt Erma took a step back and sized it up. "Not bad," she said with a curt nod. "Next we'll work on making the perfect facial expression."

"Great, can't wait," I said a little flatly.

I stopped by the nursing home that afternoon.

Lacy at the front desk greeted me with her ever-bright smile. "Henry isn't here right now, but I can let him know you stopped by."

"That's okay." I tried to match her brightness. "I'm actually looking for Bernie."

"Oh." Her eyebrows shot up. "I think she's in the dining room."

I made my way through the orange-blossom-scented hallway, shedding my jacket, hat and mittens before arriving at the doorway to the dining room. It was filled with residents playing cards, chatting, and watching the fireplace. I spotted Bernie at a table in the corner. Her perfectly curled ringlets stuck out around the edges of the book she was reading. I greeted everyone as I made my way through the room. I sat down in a chair across from her and waited for her to notice me.

She looked up, confused, as though I'd interrupted her from her deep thoughts. Bernie was sometimes able to see things that other people couldn't. It was her special brand of magic. I hadn't met anyone else yet who could do that. Her messages were usually cryptic. When Aunt Erma had been a cat, Bernie had told me several times to "dust the cat". It had taken me a while to figure out that she'd meant I should put fairy dust on the cat, but when it had all clicked in my mind I'd been able to turn Aunt Erma back into a person.

This time the situation was not quite as dramatic, but the stakes still felt pretty high to me. I wanted her to tell me if I should stay in Hocus Hills or move back to the city. I knew Lena had told me to look inside myself, but it didn't hurt to have a little outside help, did it?

"Sorry to bother you," I said. She looked at me through her large thick glasses that made her eyes look huge and blinked a few times before smiling.

"You're never a bother."

"Can I ask you something?" She put a bookmark in her book and set it on the table, then looked at me expectantly. I went through my whole dilemma with her. I covered just about every aspect of staying in Hocus Hills or going back to the city. I was very careful not to mention Henry or Josh. No one else was sitting near our table, but I didn't really want Henry to catch wind that he was both a positive and a negative in my life plans. Something about the way Bernie squinted at me made me think she already knew anyway.

"What's the right decision?" I asked her when I got all done.

"I'm not a Magic 8 Ball, dear," she said. "You can't just ask me a question, shake me, and get an answer."

"You're right, I'm sorry." It was silent for a minute while I looked around the room before turning back to her.

"Do you want to know a fun spell?" she asked, as though offering me a consolation prize for her lack of answers.

"Sure." I tried to hide my disappointment.

"Hold your ear." She demonstrated, grabbing the edge of her ear, and I copied her. "Then look at people having a conversation that you want to hear, and repeat after me."

I looked across the room to Frank Labelle and Claire Sprinkles, and repeated the spell Bernie recited. I heard the faint sound of popcorn popping. Then something strange happened. I sat up straighter in my chair as I heard Claire's voice in my ear, even though she wasn't talking to me.

"I can show you that new move I've been working on." She spoke in a low, seductive voice.

"I'll come by after everyone's in bed," he said.

"Great, see you at eight thirty." She got up with a swish of her hips and walked away.

My mouth dropped open and I turned back to Bernie. I could see her lips were moving, but I couldn't hear her. I felt panicked. Did I do the spell wrong? Had I lost my hearing? She reached over and pulled my fingers off my earlobe and I let out a breath of relief when I could hear her voice again.

"Pretty neat, isn't it?" she asked with a mischievous wiggle of her eyebrows.

I laughed and nodded, giddy with my new power. I'd completely forgotten about my original intention for coming here.

"I like to keep apprised of the goings-on here," she said.

My phone buzzed with a text from Aunt Erma asking when I'd be back.

"I better get going," I said, reluctantly standing.

She grabbed my hand tightly.

"Let the chopsticks fall," she said in the low voice she used when making a proclamation.

"What?" This was even stranger than, "Dust the cat."

"Let the chopsticks fall," she repeated, with no further helpful information.

"I don't understand what that means."

She looked at me, blinking a few times, and shrugged. "That's all I got, kid."

My phone buzzed again. This time it was my mother.

"It's busy here." I could hear her annoyed tone just in those three words. I sighed.

"Thanks, Bernie. I have to get going."

She waved and opened up her book again, but I saw her put her fingers to her ear and murmur to herself before I left. She would probably be reading that book for a while if she spent all her time eavesdropping.

During my walk back to the pie shop, I tried to figure out what Bernie had meant. How was what she said going to help me decide where to live? I'd been hoping for more specific help, even though I knew that wasn't exactly how it worked.

I tried to remember the last time I'd used chopsticks. Maybe there was a clue there. But I couldn't remember. I was the person who usually stabbed at her food until someone brought her a fork. Maybe it would come to me at the perfect moment if I was just patient. I wasn't feeling particularly patient though.

Later that night in the apartment, I was decorating the Christmas tree with my mom and Aunt Erma. As was to be expected, Aunt Erma had boxes and boxes of decorations. She was a little short on the tree though. The tree stood only about shoulder height to me.

"How are we going to fit all these decorations on that tiny thing?" my mother asked.

"Don't worry, they'll fit," Aunt Erma said. She disappeared into the kitchen.

"So, Josh is back," my mother said, unwrapping the first ornament. It was a Christmas fairy with a red sparkly dress and gold wings.

"Yes," I said. I focused all my attention on opening a box of silver and red shiny ornaments. I could feel my mother's eyes boring into me, but I kept my head down and examined the baubles with more enthusiasm than I'd ever examined any Christmas decoration before.

I screeched and threw the red ball I had been holding onto the ground. It shattered, and pieces flew across the wood floor. Mitzy came running over to see what was wrong.

"No, Mitzy," I cried, picking her up so she didn't cut her paws on the sharp bits.

"What's wrong?" my mom asked. Aunt Erma rushed in from the kitchen.

"I saw. I saw ..." I pointed to the broken pieces, clutching Mitzy so tightly she began to squirm in my arms. I couldn't say it out loud. It sounded absolutely insane.

"What did you see?" Aunt Erma asked. She put her arm around me and led me over to the sofa.

"I saw Brenda's face in the reflection of the ball," I said. Yup, it sounded crazy. My heart was pounding from my chest to my ears. "It had to be my imagination, right?" I looked to my mother and Aunt Erma for reassurance, but instead of giving it to me they were exchanging concerned glances. "That's not possible, right?" I asked again.

"It's possible," Aunt Erma said.

"But it's not good," my mom said.

"She was actually looking at me?" I asked. My voice was getting higher, almost reaching a hysterical pitch now. Mitzy finally squirmed her way out of my arms and onto the floor in front of me. She gave me an indignant sigh before trotting off to her bed in the corner.

"I'm afraid so," Aunt Erma said. "It's a very powerful magic. It takes a lot of energy and a lot of special ingredients that I don't know where she would have gotten. I'm worried she might have more help than we thought."

"Didn't you say that their son ... what was his name? Flan? Dan?" My mother snapped her fingers.

"Stan," I said.

"Right," she said, pointing at me. "Didn't you say that Stan was a delivery man? Maybe he became a delivery man wherever they're living now. Or maybe he stocked up on ingredients while he was traveling around town here. A delivery man gets a fair amount of access."

I remembered Stan looking in the cupboards of the kitchen when he was trying to find Aunt Erma's secret spices last month. I shuddered a little when I thought about how often he and I had been in the kitchen alone.

"It's okay," Aunt Erma said, patting my arm. "She's gone now."

I went over to the boxes of decorations and examined anything with a reflective surface. The only thing I saw was my own round face and curly hair as I stared intently, waiting for her face to appear.

"She's not there," my mother said.

"She probably focused all of her magic on that ball. Now that it's broken she won't have a way in for a while," Aunt Erma said.

I wanted to believe her, but I put the boxes of baubles in the back of the closet, jamming them behind all the jackets and sweaters. I pushed a chair in front of the door too, just in case.

"Here, have some hot chocolate." Aunt Erma disappeared into the kitchen and returned carrying a tray of red mugs full of steaming liquid. I took a mug and felt the heat on my hands. I inhaled the hot chocolate. The peppermint smell made my nose tingle. The first sip warmed me all the way to my toes.

"I put a little something in there," Aunt Erma said.

"A special spice?" I asked.

"No, a special schnapps," she said.

Staring at the beautifully decorated Christmas tree just didn't give me the usual joy. Aunt Erma set the lights to sparkle in time to the Christmas music we had playing, but even that didn't make me feel better.

Chapter 5

Dear Elodie,

I recently got married and discovered that my wife reuses coffee grounds. It would be bad enough if she did it just when she made coffee for us because ew, gross, right? But she also does it when she makes coffee for company. I'm all for recycling, but we have the money to use fresh coffee grounds every time we make a pot of coffee. I've tried talking to her about it, and she laughs it off. But I've seen the repulsed looks from our company, and I'm afraid people won't come to our house anymore.

Sincerely,
Grossed-out Grounds

Dear Grossed-out Grounds,

You're right, ew. If talking to your wife didn't work, my best recommendation is to make the coffee yourself. Congratulations on your recent marriage!

Ask and I'll Answer,

Elodie

"Do you want another magic lesson?" Aunt Erma asked. It had been quiet for awhile, with no magical attacks and no faces appearing where they shouldn't, but there was still a strange energy in the air. We clung to our normal routines and tried not to jump any time the phone rang.

"Yes, please," I said. I hopped up off the sofa and sent Holly a quick message. "Gotta run. Got some pie learning to do." She and I had been texting each other while we watched the same reality show. As usual, the word "reality" was used loosely here, but, after only a few weeks of watching, I found myself far too involved in the lives of the contestants to care. "Tell me how it ends," I couldn't help but add.

With everything going on, the more magic I knew, the better. We'd been trying to sneak in as many magic lessons as possible, but it was hard to work them in when we were so busy with holiday orders.

"Will you teach me how to do an attack spell?" I asked.

Aunt Erma pursed her lips together. "That's not the kind of magic we do."

"But we might need it."

"I am teaching you pie magic," she said.

"Can't you put something magical to knock out your enemies in a pie?"

"There will be no baking with hate in my pie shop." She turned on her heel and marched off. I sighed and followed her downstairs.

With my mother here, time for magic lessons was even

more scarce. She loudly sighed and banged dishes around in the kitchen whenever Aunt Erma or I brought up the topic. Her palpable disapproval made for a tough learning environment.

Aunt Erma told me that my mother used to practice magic regularly, but I never saw that side of her. Even after we reconnected with Aunt Erma, she was still reluctant to embrace magic again. I think she blamed magic for failing her when my dad was sick. She'd wanted Aunt Erma, who had always been the most powerful one in the family, to help my dad, but she'd refused. She'd said the magic for that was too dangerous. My mother had cut her out of our lives after my dad died, and neither of us saw Aunt Erma for over twenty years. Now we were trying to piece our family back together. As often was the case with family matters, we were taking steps forwards and backwards, but at least we were doing it together now.

Aunt Erma and I were both in our pajamas. She wore a rainbow-striped fleece onesie, and I had on red flannel pants and a white T-shirt that said, "Bring me coffee, or else ..." My dark curly hair was piled on my head and Aunt Erma's gray curls hung loose around her shoulders. She made both of us put on hair nets and aprons before she pulled a ball of pie-crust dough out of the fridge. Many times she'd assured me that there was a huge difference between the taste of a well-chilled pie crust and a room-temperature pie crust. A few times when Aunt Erma wasn't watching, though, I'd made pies without chilling the crust thoroughly. I couldn't tell the difference, but she always noticed and then she would proceed to lecture me for ten minutes on the importance of keeping up standards at Erma's Pie Shop.

"Erma is not only my name, it's my brand." She always began the lectures the same way. "If our standards slip, our customers will split. We don't want to leave any room for a new dessert establishment to open up in town. No more cookie shops." She would shake her head emphatically, and I'd promise to chill the crust ingredients next time.

"Let's make a banana cream tonight. Doesn't that sound good?" she asked, handing me the pie crust. I agreed and got to work rolling the crust out while she gathered the rest of the ingredients. I never ceased to be amazed by how many recipes she had memorized. I was lucky if I could remember two ingredients before I had to check a written recipe. Aunt Erma assured me that I would get the hang of it eventually, but I often just felt incompetent next to her in the kitchen.

As she disappeared into the pantry, my phone beeped with a text message. I couldn't help but glance at the screen. That was another one of Aunt Erma's rules. No technology while baking because it might distract you from the magic.

It was from Josh. "Are you around?"

I peeked around the corner to the front of the pie shop. Through the darkness I could make out his curly-haired silhouette standing by the door.

"Um, my friend Josh is here," I said.

Aunt Erma stuck her head out of the pantry with her eyebrows raised. "Well, you'd better let him in and see what he wants."

I flicked the light switch, startling Josh, who looked up from his phone. His face lit up when he saw me coming towards the door. I couldn't help but smile even though a knot was forming in my stomach. Was he back to profess his love for me? I wasn't ready for this conversation yet.

I unlocked the door and held it open.

"Hey." He hesitated, studying my face.

"Come in, it's cold," I said.

Once inside he became very interested in looking at a picture of the Morning Pie Crew that hung on the wall.

"What's up?" I asked after the silence had dragged on too long.

Aunt Erma began to hum Christmas songs from the kitchen.

Josh finally looked at me. "Nice outfit," he said.

I looked down at my pajamas and purple sparkly apron and struck a pose. "You know me, I'm such a fashion icon." He let out a breath and smiled, looking relieved. It felt as if we'd made an unspoken agreement to ignore our earlier conversation for the time being.

"I'm running into a bit of a problem with the light fixtures."

"What?"

"On the project. The owner wants these antique fixtures

put in. The wiring's weird. The mounting is weird. No one can get it right, but I know you'd be able to."

I looked into his eyes, searching for an ulterior motive, but I didn't see one.

"Isn't there an electrician on the job?" I asked.

"He's on another project and doesn't come until next week. The owners are breathing down my neck. Could you come take a look at it?" He batted his eyelashes at me. "Please Z?" I froze. Josh was the only person who ever called me Z. I used to tease him that Susie was too much of a mouthful for him. Something about the way he said it now felt more intimate than it used to. I glanced toward the kitchen. Aunt Erma was humming louder.

As though sensing my hesitation he told me more about the project. I began to imagine different possibilities for hanging the light fixtures, and I longed for the satisfaction I got from doing a job that came so naturally to me.

I threw my hands up in surrender. "Yeah, I'll stop by. Quit begging."

He beamed and gave me directions to the job site.

On his way out the door, Josh turned towards me and opened his mouth. Then he glanced over my shoulder. I followed his gaze and saw Aunt Erma openly staring from the kitchen.

"Well, goodnight. Sorry to intrude." He nodded to Aunt Erma and was gone. I let out a breath.

I smiled at Aunt Erma. "Were you listening in?"

"Well, I never!" She put her hand to her chest as though

appalled at my accusations. "I didn't hear a single word you two said." And then without missing a beat, she added, "So you're going to his job site tomorrow?"

I shrugged and went back to the half-rolled-out pie crust in the kitchen. "He needs my help."

"He needs something all right," she grumbled, and I shot her a look.

"I won't be gone long," I promised.

I heard her muttering as she retrieved her box of magic spices from its hiding place behind a secret trapdoor in the back of the pantry. She had put even more protection spells on them to keep them safe from the IMPs. She hadn't replaced the latest two bottles that Brenda had stolen.

She caught me staring at the empty slots where number seven and number nine used to sit in the box.

"They're not going to get any more. I just haven't gotten around to making new batches."

My stomach flipped when I realized she was lying to me.

She pulled out a bottle and distracted me with a quiz. "What does this one do?"

She went through the bottles, and I was getting most of them right. Laughter, encouragement, helpfulness, relaxation, love.

She was holding up spice number eight now. I wrinkled my nose as I tried to remember what that one did.

"Honesty," she said when it became apparent I didn't have the answer.

"Right," I said, slapping my hand against the kitchen island. "That one can get you into trouble."

"Yes, you have to use it very carefully and in very small amounts. It's good for people who need to stand up to someone or get in touch with their feelings," she said.

I nodded as I put the pie crust in the oven to bake.

"Tonight, I think we should try mixing two spices together. That really takes some artistry." She wiggled her eyebrows at me. "Which two should we try?"

I picked laughter and encouragement. I felt as if we could use both of those things right now.

We used instant pudding mix to make the filling of the banana cream tonight. Aunt Erma usually turned her nose up at such a shortcut, but she made an exception because it was late, and we were hungry.

"Here, put one dash of each spice in the filling," Aunt Erma said, handing me the two bottles. "Remember, your intention as you add the spice is just as important as the spice you use." There was a knock at the back door and Aunt Erma went to answer it.

We had talked about the importance of intention before, so I focused all my energy on laughter and encouragement as I sprinkled the spices into the filling.

"I heard rumors there might be some pie to try in here?" I heard Holly's voice.

"Almost ready," I called.

"I considered your text to be an invitation." She took off her coat, which she had thrown on over her purple silk pajama set, and surveyed the work we'd done. Her wild frizzy blonde hair was pulled back by a thick purple headband. "I'll make the whipped cream," she offered, washing her hands.

"Who ended up together?" I asked. I was dying to hear what had happened next on the reality show we had been watching.

"Ben kissed Cici even though Matt is clearly in love with her, and Eddie asked Julie out on a date, but the show ended before she answered."

"No!" I said. "I can't wait a whole week to find out!"

Aunt Erma watched this exchange with raised eyebrows.

"Trust me, it's an addictive show," Holly told her. "You should watch next week."

"I'm probably going to be busy," Aunt Erma said.

As we let the pie chill in the fridge, Holly told us about some of her early magic memories. She had a slow, thoughtful way of talking. "My mother always taught me growing magic because she likes to grow fresh herbs and vegetables. Our garden always grew so many vegetables, and she would send me to school with bagged lunches packed full of green things. I would con my friends out of pieces of candy, and then I would use the growing magic to make the pieces of candy ever so slightly bigger." She gave a satisfied nod. "I was quite the rebel."

"I didn't know you were such a wild child." I laughed.

Henry called, and I stepped into the dark front of the pie shop to answer it.

We talked about our days and made plans for the following day. I paced around, running my hand over the edges of tables and chairs.

"I'm helping my friend Josh at his job site," I said. There was a pause on the other end of the phone. "You still there?"

"Yeah, that's great," he said evenly.

"It's the light fixtures. Light's important, you know," I babbled. "The day doesn't end when the sun goes down."

I bit my tongue as I stubbed my toe on the bookshelf by the window.

"Have fun. I have to go walk Willy now," Henry said. I heard Willy gently woofing in the background.

"Okay, bye." I tried to shake the weird feeling from the phone call as I headed back to the bright kitchen.

We didn't let the pie chill in the fridge for long before we cut large slices for each of us.

Aunt Erma took the first bite and let out a giggle. "I think you may have put a bit too much of the laughter spice in here," she said.

"I think you did a great job," Holly said after her first bite. "Really top notch. No one can spice a pie like you can. We should crown you pie-spicing queen of the universe." She yelled the last part and we all collapsed into a pile of giggles.

"Did I put in too much of the encouragement too?" I asked.

"Yes," Aunt Erma snorted. "But we can try again tomorrow."

"I'll be back for that," Holly said. She put her face really close to mine until her light blue eyes were gazing deep into my own dark blue ones. "You're an amazing best friend and I know you'll do even better tomorrow, but you did a pretty spectacular job today."

"Thanks, Hol." I gave her a hug. It didn't matter that it was the spices talking. I'd really needed to hear that today.

I wanted to join the fun, so I took a bite of pie. It was quite tasty. We alternated between gushing over each other's fabulous qualities and laughing hysterically.

There was still room for improvement in my magical education, but the learning process sure was fun.

Chapter 6

Dear Elodie,

I have a very serious relationship problem. I've been with this guy for a few weeks, and it has been wonderful. He really is everything I could have ever wanted. My problem is that this other guy has come out of the woodwork and said he is in love with me too. I've been single for a long time. Where was this guy then? He had been around for years just twiddling his thumbs not saying anything, and then now, when I'm happy and with someone new, he steps to center stage with some dramatic proclamation. I don't know what to do. He's not that great of a guy, but I don't want to hurt his feelings. How do I get him out of here and get back to my prince without hurting the other guy's feelings? I never thought I'd be in a love triangle, and when I did dream about it, I didn't imagine it would be so hard.

Sincerely,
Everyone Loves Me

Dear Everyone Loves Me,

Clearly you have to send the other guy packing as soon as possible. It sounds like you're with the right guy now. Why would the other guy choose this time to reveal his feelings? Some men always want what they can't have, and this seems like a classic case of that. I think you should tell him to go away and not come back. If he had really loved you, he would not have popped back into your life like this.

Ask and I'll Answer,

Elodie

I stormed into the nursing home, barely acknowledging Lacy, the woman behind the front counter.

"Henry's in the dining room," she called.

"Thanks," I said over my shoulder, not slowing down. He was sitting at a table playing cards with a few of the residents.

"Can I talk to you?" I asked him through clenched teeth, not even saying hi to the other people. They looked at him with raised eyebrows, and he looked a little sheepish.

"Sure," he said, slowly getting up. "I'll be right back. No peeking at my cards, Mr. Gary," he said.

Mr. Gary gave him a wide-eyed innocent look through his thick-rimmed glasses. "I'm no cheater," he said. "You're just a terrible player."

The table cracked up, and Henry followed me outside.

"I'm guessing you've read today's paper," he said, ducking his head.

"Yes," I said, crossing my arms. "Care to explain, oh my royal prince." He grimaced.

"Yeah, I wrote that when I was upset. I probably should have waited and read it after I had calmed down before sending it to my editor," he said.

"Ya think?" I asked.

"You have to understand this is hard for me too," he said, rubbing his forehead.

"And that gives you the right to publish this?" I held up the newspaper. I wasn't ready to let him off the hook.

"No, you're right. I shouldn't have said it. I'm really sorry. I know you're actually going through a hard time, and I know Josh is too," he added reluctantly. "I just really like you."

"You think that's an excuse?" I asked.

"No, of course not," he said. "I made a mistake."

"Just please don't use my personal life in your column again," I said. His apologies and big brown eyes were making my boiling anger cool to a simmer.

"Deal," he said, reaching out his hand. I shook it. "Unless it's something really juicy," he added with a twinkle in his eye. I gently punched his shoulder.

"Maybe I'll start writing a competing advice column."

I tapped my finger on my lip, thoughtfully. "What will the first column be about? Maybe something about a guy who claims to love fruitcake, but actually just stores it in a chest freezer in his basement whenever people give it to him."

His eyes widened. "You wouldn't! There would be a mutiny here." He carefully took the newspaper out of my hand. "Maybe I can hold onto this," he said. "So you don't do anything crazy, like reread this garbage." I let him have it because he was probably right. If I read it again, I'd get angry again.

Well, I thought as I walked away and headed back to the pie shop, Henry and I had survived our first fight. And since I was the winner, I thought it went well. I wondered if Henry would be able to keep his anonymity as Elodie with such a blatant letter. It was so obviously about me and Josh and Henry. Wouldn't everyone be able to see that?

It turned out it was easy for them to miss the signs. The Morning Pie Crew talked about Ask Elodie, as they usually did, but they didn't say anything about me and Henry. Were they being polite? I considered the possibility, but then I thought, who am I kidding? The Morning Pie Crew never bothered to be polite or respect my privacy. After my and Henry's fourth date, Lena wiggled her eyebrows at me and asked if Henry had "frosted my cupcakes".

"Remember that time Lionel proclaimed his love for Flora?" Lena asked.

"Right!" Aunt Erma's eyes lit up. "He came in here and read a poem to the whole pie shop!"

I could see Lena was trying not to laugh. Flora just focused on her slice of pecan pie as though she couldn't even hear them.

"My favorite line was, 'Oh, my sweet, beautiful Flora-boo, I really do adore-a you.'" Lena threw her head back and cackled.

"I thought it was so romantic." Mr. Barnes sighed.

"It would have been far more romantic if I was the only person he'd done that to," Flora said.

"What?" I asked.

"Unfortunately he also used the same poem to proclaim his love to Nora and Cora." She gave her patented disapproving Flora look.

"He was playing the odds," Lena said, then shrank back when Flora turned her look on her. "Despicable," she added.

I checked all the tools in my bag. I knew they were all there because I kept them in the trunk of my car. I only took them out to use them and clean them. I remembered as a child my father sitting at the kitchen table cleaning his tools.

My mother would always scold him. "Can't you do that in the garage?"

He would just give her his charming smile and look at her with his big twinkling eyes and her expression would soften and she'd walk away.

I loved to help him. I was always fascinated by these pieces of metal that were so important to him.

"Take care of your tools and they'll take care of you," he'd tell me.

He'd hand me a soft worn rag and let me polish them. He'd let me tell him all about my day without interruption. When my mother would say it was almost time for bed, we'd put the tools down and have a snack. Usually pie Aunt Erma had made or sometimes ice cream from a local creamery that my dad would pick up on his way home from work. He would always get the one that had large chunks of peanut butter cup, my favorite. Whenever my dad ate ice cream, some would end up on his mustache and I would laugh hysterically as he twisted his face into silly expressions as he tried to lick it off.

I looked over the directions Josh had sent me and headed to the job site. I felt a familiar rush of excitement as I pulled up in front of a house surrounded by work trucks and a dumpster out front. I loved these big projects. Watching a building transform from run-down and forgotten to updated and cared for.

Josh appeared next to my car, bouncing on his toes before I'd even opened the door.

"Someone's had his coffee this morning," I said, smiling.

He shrugged. "I'm in a good mood. It's a beautiful day!"

I looked up at the gray sky with raised eyebrows.

"Come on, I'll show you around."

It really was an extensive project. He introduced me to

a few people as we walked through, who nodded in my direction before getting back to work. Finally he showed me the light fixtures. There were four of them, each one a little different. All of them had pieces of twisted brass tube running from the base and spinning out in different directions with several light bulbs hanging off the edges of the brass.

Josh grabbed a ladder and set it up where the first light fixture would go.

"Wow, these are unique," I said. I circled them, already forming a plan on how to best hang them. I could feel Josh's eyes on me. "I know you have a lot to do. I got this," I said.

"Okay," he said reluctantly. "Just holler if you need anything."

I quickly got lost in my work – it was nice to not think about magic or the IMPs or even Josh and Henry for a while – and it wasn't until I heard a crash that I was startled out of my wiring reverie.

"Sorry, so sorry." I stopped breathing as I heard a faint but familiar voice coming from the front of the house. I slowly climbed down off the ladder, clutching a screwdriver tightly in my hand. I had to see. Maybe it wasn't him. But what if it was him and he wasn't alone?

I peered through the doorway, hoping I wouldn't see him. I just wanted to get back to light fixtures and wires.

Well, crap. I saw his nervous figure on his hands and

knees scooping up boxes of screws while a frustrated man tried to shoo him away.

"It's fine. I got it," the other man said as Stan continued to apologize.

I quickly looked around the rest of the room? Was anyone else there? Brenda? I figured I would feel her eyes boring a hole in the wall if she was around. It looked as if Stan had come alone. I needed to find out why. Was he delivering something? He used to be the delivery man in Hocus Hills, maybe he found a new job in this town. Maybe he could tell me what his parents were planning. I knew Violet would be livid if I didn't call her immediately, but I couldn't let him leave without talking to him.

I approached slowly as though afraid I would startle him and he would run. My heart was racing. I hadn't seen him since I'd found out he was working with Alice. I'd always thought he was just the clumsy delivery guy. His floppy hair was even shaggier than I remembered.

I was almost on top of him before he noticed me. He froze, his eyes wide. I felt my own muscles tense, ready to tackle him if he tried to run.

"Stan," I said. I was relieved my voice came out sounding fairly calm.

I could practically see the wheels turning in his head. He was probably trying to figure out how to play this. Maybe he would pretend he didn't know me, or pretend he wasn't Stan. What if he tried to attack me? That didn't seem like Stan's style, especially with so many witnesses, but he had been hanging out with his mother lately. That could be enough to turn anyone into a raving lunatic. The silence dragged on so long I finally added, "Can we talk?"

He slowly stood, and I grabbed his arm. The frustrated man who was still picking up his screws looked at us with raised eyebrows.

"We're old friends," I said with a bright smile. I led Stan out to the yard through the snow until we were alone next to a big pine tree. "What are you doing here?" I snapped.

"I should be asking you the same thing." I think he meant to sound tough, but he came across sounding more like a sullen teenager instead.

"Are your parents here?"

"They might be nearby." His gaze shifted from my shoes to over my shoulder and I resisted the urge to follow it. If Dennis and Brenda were standing behind me, I was pretty sure I would feel them.

"What is the plan with the spices?" I leaned in, still gripping his arm.

He glanced down at my hand and I realized I was still holding the screwdriver.

I pointed the end toward him. "Well?" I asked, lowering my voice in an attempt to sound menacing. I could feel Stan start to shake.

"I don't ... I can't ..." he stuttered. This was far less satisfying than I was hoping for. I almost felt bad for him, but I remembered what we were fighting for. Whether or not his mother was a bully, he was still helping her and that still made him the enemy.

"Come on, Stan." I sweetened my voice and lowered the screwdriver. "Don't you want to do the right thing?" His eyes met mine for a split second.

"I can't. Ivan would kill me," he said softly.

"Who's Ivan?" The remaining color from Stan's already pale complexion drained from his face.

"Z, what are you doing?" Josh was walking towards us. I dropped Stan's arm. He was gone before I could get out another word. For a clumsy guy, he could move fast.

"Listen, Josh, I'm sorry, but I really have to go." I felt a twinge of guilt thinking about the two other light fixtures still sitting on the floor.

"Is everything okay?" He followed me to my car.

"I'll call you later."

I called Violet first, then Aunt Erma. Violet was curt and demanding, as usual. Aunt Erma got strangely quiet after hearing about my encounter.

"I'll be back soon," I told her. I felt anxiety swell after I hung up. I'd been ready for a lot of different reactions from Aunt Erma, but silence wasn't one of them.

Violet was waiting at the pie shop when I got back, ready to ask more questions.

"Did it look like he had the spices with him?"

"Well, I didn't check his pockets, but I don't think so."

"You didn't see any evidence of magic?" She was holding a notebook with a pen poised over the page. I wracked my brain, wishing I could give her something more, anything. Everything at the job site had seemed fine, but I hadn't exactly been keeping an eye out for the Drakes to appear.

"Will Josh be okay?" The last thing I wanted was to somehow drag him into this crazy world. I couldn't even imagine his reaction if I said, "Hey, magic is real and this crazy magic family is trying to steal all of Aunt Erma's special spices so they can take over the world. So maybe keep an eye out."

"He should be fine. We have some Magic Enforcement Officers stationed around the house now." She turned to leave.

"Will you let me know if you find Stan?" I asked. She gave me a distracted nod and was gone.

It was a small spell. One I had been practicing with hit or miss success for the last couple weeks. Aunt Erma showed me the words to say from one of Flora's books, and I repeated them until I had them memorized.

It was just supposed to brush all the crumbs off all the tables so I could easily sweep them off the floor. The magical cleaners came every night, though I'd still never seen them, only their handiwork, but we still had to keep the pie shop presentable during the day. There was also a spell to sweep up the crumbs, but I hadn't learned it yet.

"That one's a bit more complicated," Aunt Erma said. I was eager to learn, but she was constantly worried about overwhelming me. So for now, I stuck to a broom and dustpan. The "old school" way.

The tables were coated with so many pie crumbs. As with any new spell, Aunt Erma had supervised me the first few times I'd done it, but today she was in the kitchen adding chocolate curls to the French Silk pies.

I focused my energy and muttered the spell.

A loud bang made me jump. The crumbs had certainly all fallen off the tables, but the pictures had all fallen off the walls and all the needles and decorations had fallen off the Christmas tree too. It looked like a sad naked stick. Aunt Erma came running out of the kitchen, her eyes wide.

"What happened?"

"I think I did it wrong." I stood frozen, surveying the damage.

We made plans to go out tree shopping. Apparently the world would end if we didn't have a Christmas tree in the front of the pie shop.

"I'm not going to be able to go with you today," Aunt Erma announced as I wrote the different pie flavors on the chalkboard.

I turned to her, trying to hide my disappointment. "Why not?"

"Violet wants me to strategize with her. There's been a

little chatter that the IMPs are going to try something again soon," she said. As much as I had been looking forward to this outing today, I couldn't argue with that. "I ran into Henry when I was at the grocery store, and he offered to go with you," she added.

"Great," I said with a forced smile. I had forgiven Henry, but I'd thought I would have another day to fully cool off before we spent too much time together. Henry entered the shop before I could try and get out of it with a "maybe we can go tomorrow" suggestion.

"Hi," Henry greeted us. He smiled at me with a hint of guilt and a bit of hope. I felt some of my frostiness melt away.

I grabbed my coat and Aunt Erma sent us off with a reminder to get a small tree.

"There's not a lot of room here, so make sure you get one that's yay big or smaller." She held her hand up to the top of her head.

We walked the short distance to the tree lot that was set up in the parking lot by the school mostly in silence. Most people had already gotten their trees since it was mid-December. The lot had just a few near the front. The leftovers had wonky branches or crooked tops and no one was manning the booth. There was just a bucket hanging in front of it with a sign that said, "Pay here."

"They're all too big," I said, looking up at one that was missing half its needles. I'd be in trouble if I brought that one back.

"I think there's more in the field back there," Henry said, disappearing behind the school. I slowly wandered after him. "Help," I heard him yell suddenly, and I ran towards the sound of his voice. I rounded the corner and saw Henry standing in an awkward position knee deep in snow. "Stop," he said when I got close.

"What's wrong?"

"The snow. I'm stuck." He moved a little and sank down a few more inches. "It's sticky. I think there's a spell on it."

"Should I call Violet?" I asked. My heart was racing as Henry went down another inch.

Henry nodded. His face was pale. He closed his eyes, and I could hear him murmuring something. A spell or a prayer. I wasn't sure.

I gave Violet a slightly hysterical account of what was happening.

"I'll be there in three minutes," she said. I wasn't sure if Henry had three minutes. He was already waist-deep.

"It's just so sticky," he said. He lifted his mittened hand up, and the snow clung to it, stringy, almost like molasses. I had an idea. Last week I had dropped a giant glass jug of maple syrup. The glass had shattered, and syrup had splattered everywhere. The puddle had spread quickly and seemed to cover every surface in the kitchen in no time, including my pants. I had been moaning about how much time it would take me to clean up all the syrup, and Aunt Erma had taught me a spell that had made the syrup not sticky. It had still been a mess to clean up, but it had just been liquid. That had made it so much easier.

I tried the spell now. I closed my eyes and focused all my energy towards Henry as I spoke the words Aunt Erma had taught me. I snapped my eyes open, not really thinking I had accomplished anything, but there was Henry, waist-deep in a puddle instead of the snow. I yanked him out of the puddle and we lay on the ground. We held each other tightly, both breathing hard.

I didn't want to let go, even as Violet and Aunt Erma appeared on the scene.

Aunt Erma ran over and threw her arms around me and Henry. "Are you two okay?" she asked, squeezing us tightly. We both nodded shakily, and told her and Violet what had happened.

"I'm going to get some Magic Enforcement Officers out here to inspect the scene," Violet said. "I think the IMPs were trying to catch Erma because she mentioned she was going tree shopping today in the pie shop."

"I'm sorry you got caught in it." Aunt Erma looked as if she might cry.

"It's okay. Susie saved me." Henry reached over to hold my hand.

"You should get inside," Violet told Henry, whose teeth were chattering. "I'll work on things here." Aunt Erma ushered us back to the pie shop, and I brought Henry upstairs to find something he could change into. I gave him a pair of fleece pants and an oversized T-shirt that I wore as pajamas sometimes. I had gotten a little wet when I was pulling him out of the puddle, so I changed into a dry pair of fleece leggings and a long blue sweatshirt.

When Henry came out of the bathroom, he came over to me and gently twisted one of my curls around his finger. "Thanks for saving my life," he said. His breath smelled minty fresh, and I had a feeling he'd just used some of my mouthwash. I was suddenly a little self-conscious of my coffee breath.

"Any time," I said out of the corner of my mouth so as not to blow my bad breath into his face. He leaned in and kissed me, long and slow. His lips were still ice cold, but I didn't mind, and he didn't seem to mind my coffee breath.

I traced the edge of his ear with my finger and kissed him again. He grasped the bottom of my sweatshirt and pulled me closer.

"We should probably get back downstairs," he said. My mind had wandered in a different direction and it took me a minute to return to reality and process what he was saying. I hated to say it, but he was right.

I groaned and let my head fall to his chest. "We're going to be stuck answering questions forever," I said.

The whole Morning Pie Crew was at the front of the shop drinking coffee when we went back downstairs. Their questions began the minute they saw us. We were about at the part where Henry was sinking in the snow when Violet showed up.

"How did you get him out of there?" she asked in her direct way. I was a little miffed that she was ruining the dramatic tension I was building up in my story, but I told her the spell I had used and why. Violet narrowed her eyes at me.

"The magic in the snow was very powerful," she said. "That spell shouldn't have worked on it."

I shrugged as everyone stared at me. "Maybe it was the adrenaline? Can that make magic stronger?" I asked.

"No," Violet said, still studying me. I shifted uncomfortably. "You just did a whole different level of magic."

I was relieved that night when Holly said she was still free to grab a drink at Sal's. I could really use a night out. I got there first, which wasn't unusual. Sal's was our one bar in town. It was dimly lit with creaky wooden floors. There was a jukebox in the front and a pool table in the back. I ordered a beer from Sal and sat near the pool table. Maybe this would be the night I discovered my super-hidden talent for pool. I hummed along to the country Christmas songs that were playing from the jukebox and stared blankly at the football game that was on TV. I was almost finished with my first beer by the time Holly rushed in.

"Sorry I'm late," she said, patting her windblown blonde hair down. "Cabbage catastrophe." Holly worked at Basil's Market, and I'd gotten used to her strange food emergencies.

She ordered a drink, something pink and fizzy, and we got right into the gossip.

"I heard you saved Henry's life," she said.

"What can I say? I'm just a regular superhero." I shrugged.

"I heard you did some pretty serious magic."

I shrugged again. "It was a pretty serious situation." I tried not to picture Henry disappearing into the sticky snow.

Holly studied my face for a minute while I studied the bubbles in my beer. She let me off the hook and moved on to lighter conversation for awhile.

By the time we were working on our second drinks, we were trying to solve the problem of the IMPs.

"Do you think Stan's evil?" I asked. I remembered the twinge of sympathy I felt when I saw him at the job site.

"I don't think he's a good person," she said, biting a cherry off the stem.

We were silent for a minute.

"How do we stop them?" I asked. I was ripping my cocktail napkin into tiny pieces.

"The IMPs?"

I nodded.

Holly gently took the napkin away from me and shrugged.

"How do we stop them?" I was ripping my cocktail napkin into tiny pieces. Holly gently took the napkin away from me and shrugged.

"We keep them from getting too much magic."

After that we moved on to solving more important problems, like whether or not Holly could catch the kernels of popcorn that I threw to her.

Chapter 7

Dear Elodie,

I think my house is haunted. I live alone and several times a week when I come home the remote control is in a different spot or a door is open that I'm sure I left closed. Whenever I buy a box of cookies, it always disappears within a couple days with nothing but a few crumbs on the bottom. It has to be ghosts, right? I tried putting up a camera so I could see them, but the camera always stops recording on the days when the ghost visits.

The only other person who has a key to my house is my neighbor. He said he's never seen anyone coming or going when I'm not home.

What should I do? Try to befriend the ghost in my house, or move?

Sincerely,
Victim of a Ghoulish Guest

Dear Victim of a Ghoulish Guest,
I would take the key back from your neighbor. If you

*don't believe me, hide a camera somewhere and don't
tell your neighbor where it is. You just might see a face
you recognize.*

　　Ask and I'll Answer,

　　　　　　　　　　　　　　　　　　Elodie

I woke up feeling unsettled. After seeing Brenda's face in the Christmas ornament a few nights ago, and Henry almost getting eaten by a pile of snow yesterday, I was worried about what today might bring. I kept checking every reflective surface to see if a face other than my own was looking back at me. I got ready quickly so I didn't have to be alone in the bathroom with the mirror for too long, and I gave the Christmas tree a wide berth.

Aunt Erma was already down in the kitchen prepping pies. No matter how early I got up, she always seemed to be up earlier. I wondered if she ever actually slept.

"How did you sleep?" she asked, examining me. I shrugged. "I need your head in the game today."

Oh right, it was the day of the snowman-building contest.

"The snow in the square is all packed down from everyone walking through and kids playing. How are they going to have enough for the contest?" I asked.

"They have snow-making machines." Aunt Erma pulled her flour-covered hands out of the bowl to do the air quotes she often used when she meant someone was going to use magic.

I helped Aunt Erma with the prep. If there was anyone

who wasn't in the Christmas spirit yet, today's choices would certainly make them feel jolly. We had a peppermint cream pie, a Ho Ho hot chocolate cream, a Rudolph's nose cherry crumble, and an elf's apple ribbon pie. We set out all the pies and unlocked the door. Aunt Erma posted a sign at the front door that announced our shortened hours for the day, but of course everyone in town already knew about them. We were going to be closed during the competition, but we would reopen afterwards so everyone could come in for a slice of pie and a nice steaming cup of coffee or hot chocolate. We served the first few early-bird customers, and then the shop emptied.

"Now sit, eat," Aunt Erma said, pushing me towards a table with a slice of pie in her hand. "You need your energy for the competition."

"To be honest, my heart just isn't really in it," I said. I felt as if I was going to be looking over my shoulder at every turn all day. I had already thought I'd seen Dennis and Brenda walk past the pie shop three times this morning. My skin prickled at the thought of being outside in the open surrounded by snow. Spells could just fly from any direction and sticky piles of magic snow could try to suck me in. Between that and wanting to win the competition for Aunt Erma I was a jumbled bundle of nerves.

"It will be fine," Aunt Erma assured me. She set a cup of coffee in front of me.

"I don't know if I can handle any more coffee," I said. My leg was already jiggling under the table.

"Don't worry, it's decaf," she said. She put her hand on my knee and firmly held it down.

I was halfway through the slice of pie when my nerves began to settle. It felt like a wave of calm that started at the top of my head and slid down until it washed over the very tips of my toes.

"What's in this pie?" I asked, a little suspiciously.

"Oh, you know, a sprinkle of this, a dash of that," she said with a wink. "Enjoy every bite, and you'll be ready for the competition."

The creamy chocolate flavor was easy to devour. I drank the coffee, and by the time we had to go outside for the competition, I had almost forgotten that we were all in terrible danger.

I could see the clouds of my breath when we went outside. Mitzy came along dressed in her Erma's Pie Shop dog coat. The coat was sparkly and red, lined with white fur, and when Mitzy wore it, she lifted her paws high in a proud prance. It had taken a week, but I wasn't embarrassed to walk with her anymore when she was wearing it. Aunt Erma was in a bright red coat with green polka dots. She wore a large hat shaped like a snowman. It had to be at least two feet high. She also carried red and green pom-poms with her.

"Pom-poms?" I asked, trying to hide my smile.

"Yes, I'm not only the sponsor, I'm also the official cheerleader," she said with a wave of the pom-poms.

I hoped she wasn't wearing a cheerleading uniform under that coat. With Aunt Erma, anything was possible.

The crowd had already begun to gather in the square. Children were throwing snowballs and making snow angels. Adults were talking and laughing with the kind of jolly animation that only seemed to come out at Christmas time. The snow was piled high. There were a couple fires burning in barrels at the edge of the sidewalk, and people huddled around the flames, holding their mittened hands out to warm them. Christmas music played from somewhere in the bundle of evergreen trees at the corner of the square. Somehow the place seemed to be covered in even more Christmas lights. The air practically sparkled with the excited energy that buzzed around. I half expected to see Santa Claus fly in on his sleigh.

Wait, there was Santa Claus – or at least Tanner O'Connell dressed up as Santa Claus. The crowd was eating it up as he walked around and took pictures with people. Several children and a few adults told him what they wanted for Christmas. Then he walked up to the steps of the gazebo. The gazebo was lined with lights that were flashing to the beat of the Christmas music that was playing. When he took the microphone and began to speak, the music died down. I didn't know if it was the outfit or magic, but his voice sounded two octaves deeper than it did most days.

"Welcome to the fifty-sixth annual snowman-building contest! This has been a proud tradition for Hocus Hills thanks to our former mayor Barney Wallace, who created this competition one drunken night," Tanner said. Barney was in his eighties now and sat covered in a blanket on a bench in the gazebo. He waved proudly to the crowd. "Every year the competition gets fiercer, and the prize gets better." He held up a large green gift bag. "I don't want to ruin the surprise, but, trust me, there are some spectacular goodies in here." I thought he was overselling it a bit since I had helped Aunt Erma put together the grand prize. It was a dozen mini pumpkin pies, a Hocus Hills T-shirt, and a mug that said, "I built the best snowman" on one side and "Hocus Hills 56th Annual Snowman Building Contest proudly sponsored by Erma's Pie Shop" on the other side. He went on to thank Erma's Pie Shop and then rambled on for another ten minutes about what a proud tradition this was for our town. I stopped listening and started planning what I wanted for lunch. I was leaning towards a grilled cheese sandwich and tomato soup. As he began to wind down, Aunt Erma grabbed my arm.

"You have to focus. Get your head in the game. Remember everything we practiced," she said. "Round balls. Make the first one large, then make the head second, and make the third one the middle so you can make it exactly the right size. You know when you make the middle second then the proportions get all off."

"I know. I remember," I said as I eyed a passer-by's steaming paper cup of hot chocolate longingly. I was as competitive as the next person. Some people, such as Josh, might say I was even more competitive than the average person. All because of one out-of-hand Pictionary incident in which I'd pulled all the cards out of the box and thrown them at him. It had been a surprisingly satisfying experience and Josh had just stared at me with wide eyes before bursting out laughing. I couldn't help it. I'd ended up laughing too. But since the prize for the snowman-building competition was a gift bag that I'd helped to make, it didn't seem as if it was worth all the determination Aunt Erma was pouring into it.

"Get ready," Santa Claus yelled into the microphone. It was so loud I cringed and plugged the ear that was closest to the speakers. "Get set." People shuffled into the places nearest the large snow piles. Then we all froze. The only sound was the wind and the occasional rustle of people's jackets. "Go-o-o-o-o-o-o-o," he yelled, and everyone sprang into action.

I wanted to watch the mayhem, but Aunt Erma was yelling at me. "Let's go let's go let's go! Get your head in the game!" I reluctantly gathered some snow in my hands to get the first ball going.

"Come on. Get rolling. Make the edges smooth," she commanded from the sidelines. "Susie." She snapped her fingers at me, and I looked at her. "You have to go faster," she said. I looked around and saw that everyone else was much further along than I was, but they also seemed to be having a lot more fun than I was.

"Isn't there some rule about not harassing the snowman makers?" I asked.

"Nope," Aunt Erma replied, not missing a beat.

"Hey, you're here." Henry rushed over to me.

"Don't distract her, Henry," Aunt Erma scolded. Aunt Erma was holding a bag full of our props for the snowman. She even included a pie tin that I was supposed to use positioned in the snowman's arms. "You have to make sure it's at a jaunty angle and that it doesn't fall. That would be horrible, if it fell," Aunt Erma had told me one day last week when we were practicing. I had broken three glass pie plates before Aunt Erma had decided we should just use an aluminum tin full of whipped cream. "It doesn't look as pretty as the glass ones, but all of the judges will be looking at the whipped cream anyway. Oh, especially if we add chocolate chips." She congratulated herself with her great idea. Then she pulled out the notebook and made a note. She had been doing that all along, making notes for me to study later.

"How are you doing?" Henry asked in a low voice. Aunt Erma, with her superhuman hearing, narrowed her eyes at him.

"Great," I said. "Building a snowman is fun." I gave him a big fake smile and an overly enthusiastic thumbs-up. He laughed.

"Violet sent me to talk to both of you, actually," he said.

Aunt Erma let out a dramatic sigh. "Okay, what is it?" she asked.

"Violet said there have been some indications that Stan has been in town," he said.

"In this town?" I felt my heart beat faster. I remembered

Stan's anxious darting eyes and his scrawny frame. He seemed harmless enough, albeit a bit of a bumbling buffoon, but, with Brenda as his mother, I knew just how dangerous he could be.

He nodded.

Aunt Erma's brow furrowed. "Does she know why? What is he trying to do?"

"She's not sure. She's trying to figure that out now. She said she just caught the faintest traces of his magic. One of the other officers picked it up, but he must have used a very good magic eraser because it disappeared quickly," he said.

"Are there any other IMPs here?" I asked.

"Not that we know of," he said.

"We'll keep our antenna up," Aunt Erma assured him.

"Good," Henry said. "I'm going to stay here and help for a while. Just to make sure nothing happens."

The adrenaline was pumping through my veins after Henry's very troubling announcement. I worked more quickly than before, packing the snow so tightly my snowman was practically an ice man. The thought of Stan back in town sent goosebumps up and down my arms. Aunt Erma seemed pleased with my new work ethic, ignoring the fact that it was motivated by fear.

"Don't worry," she said. "The whole town is here. They wouldn't dare try anything today. Too many magical people around." She said the last part in a low voice as there were a lot of tourists who came for the contest.

I struggled with the snowman's face, trying to arrange the knick-knacks we'd assembled into the perfect "welcoming expression" that Aunt Erma was aiming for. First it looked angry, then surprised, then confused, and finally, after a few more tweaks, I ended up with a look that passed inspection.

I dressed the snowman in an apron and managed to put the whipped-cream pie on the stick arm perfectly. Okay, maybe it took me a few tries, but still, it seemed to stay. And more importantly, Aunt Erma seemed happy. She circled the snowman a couple times, nodding approvingly. Henry helped me stick two poles in the ground behind the snowman – stretched between them was a banner that read, "Erma's Pies, stop by for a slice after the competition. All entrants will receive ten per cent off a slice of pie."

I looked around and marveled at the artistry of the other creations. I had never before realized that snowmen could be more than just three balls with some coal eyes and a carrot nose. These were amazing. "Frosty the Snowman" began to play from the speakers indicating the end of the competition, and Aunt Erma started singing along. Henry joined her and soon all the people surrounding us were singing. I tried to sing too, but I had a lump at the back of my throat. There was something special about a group of people singing together that made me emotional. It really brought people together. We were a community. All a little strange, but all of us were doing this same crazy project. Even the tourists were part of our beautiful small town of Hocus Hills even if just for today. I couldn't leave this.

I jumped when I felt something poke my ribs. I turned, expecting to see Henry, but it was the arm of the snowman jabbing me. Was Aunt Erma using magic on the snowman? I thought they said they waited until after all the tourists had left to do that kind of magic. I looked over at Aunt Erma to see what the heck was going on. The look on her face made it clear she wasn't the one using magic. Then everything went white as the snowman hurled the tin of whipped cream at my face.

There was a moment where I was frozen with shock. I heard the commotion begin around me. People yelling. Lots of alarmed voices crying out, "What's happening?" I frantically wiped the whipped cream away from my face. When I had finally cleared it from my eyes, I saw Aunt Erma and Henry trying to cast spells in the direction of the snowmen, but they didn't seem to stop them. Henry was right next to me, his hand on my back.

"Are you okay?" he asked. He glanced at me, his brow furrowed.

"Fine," I said. Henry turned back to try and stop a snowman that was trying to roll over a man who danced around to avoid being squished.

I listened to the words Henry was saying and repeated them. I wasn't exactly sure what the spell was supposed to do, but I tried to imagine the snowmen melting as I said it. It wasn't any more effective for me than it was for him though. The psychotic snowmen barely reacted when hit by the spell.

It was easy to spot the tourists. They were the ones with confused terror on their faces, running and hiding. I could only imagine what it would be like to plan a day of family fun only to be attacked by Frosty the Snowman. It was strange, though – the snowmen didn't seem to target the tourists. In fact, they seemed to be targeting very specific residents of Hocus Hills. Aunt Erma chased after a snowman who was swinging a broom at Lena.

A woman's voice came on over the speaker, singing along loudly to the Christmas music. My blood ran cold. It was Brenda's voice. "Tired of keeping your magic hidden? Being yourself has always been forbidden? Join a great cause. Let's lighten the laws. It's time we see Improvement for Magical People!"

The Magic Enforcement Officers arrived and cleared the square of all non-magical people. I wondered how this would be explained to them. Would they try to convince them it was just an elaborate prank? As someone who was still pretty new to this magic thing, I completely understood their panic. Every day I was surprised by something I learned about magic. Some days it was something fun, like you could listen in on conversations across the room. Other days it was less fun, like there was a power-hungry group who wanted to cause chaos and steal Aunt Erma's magic.

The annoying song about joining the IMPs was playing

on repeat over the speaker. I wished I could find the speakers and smash them with a bat.

"It's not working," I wailed breathlessly as two more snowmen rolled towards me and Henry.

Mr. Barnes, Lena, and Flora rushed over. Along the way, Mr. Barnes had to dodge a rolling snowman whose thrashing stick arms came within inches of his face.

A snowman dressed like a witch was coming towards me waving its broom. I yelled the spell with all my might, and the snowman only stumbled, but it dropped the broom.

I lunged for it. I felt his frozen body pressing against me, and I struggled to hold onto the stick end of the broom over my head.

"What are you doing?" Henry yelled, sounding shocked and panicked.

I was too busy wrestling with the snowman to answer. We were rolling on the ground now. I gripped the handle tightly with both hands as I tried to kick the icy round balls off me. I came away triumphantly with just a few scratches and the broom in my hands.

"They're just a bunch of frozen droplets of water," I said, recognizing the irony, considering how Henry was almost killed by a bunch of frozen droplets of water just yesterday. Then I lifted the broom above my head and swung it down on the snowman, turning it back into a pile of snow.

The others got on board quickly, using anything they could find to smash the snowmen. Tanner was using the bag of presents that was part of his Santa costume to bludgeon a snowman who looked like a cartoon bear. Lena had found a plastic sword and was taking out snowmen while yelling, "En garde. Take that, and that, and that," with every swing.

In no time, all the snowmen had been reduced to piles of snow, and the square was littered with props. In the chaos, someone had successfully smashed the speakers and the singing had stopped. It was silent for a moment. I couldn't hear anything but my heavy breathing.

"Well, everyone." Violet stood on the steps of the gazebo. I'm not even sure when she got there. "That was more excitement than we bargained for today." She was trying to keep her tone light. "Thank you all for your hard work here. The IMPs have been acting out, but we have it under control."

"This didn't look like it was under control," someone from the crowd yelled.

"There were a lot of outsiders here today. What are you going to do about that?" another voice called.

"We're sending some teams out to take care of that," Violet said calmly.

"I think some of them have left already," someone said.

"Can you blame them?" another voice added. "They just saw a whole passel of snowmen come to life."

"We're going to take care of them too," Violet said. "By tomorrow, they will all think they've just had a very strange dream." This seemed to be a pattern, and I began to wonder how many of my strange dreams had actually happened. Had I once really fallen out of a boat and been rescued by a mermaid, or was that just a dream? I tried to make a mental note to ask Aunt Erma that very question next time we had a chance to talk. "As for right now, everyone should just go home and be with your families," Violet continued. "Keep your eyes and ears open, and report anything strange you might see to the Magic Enforcement Officers immediately."

The crowd dispersed, and I followed the Morning Pie Crew, Aunt Erma, and Henry back to the pie shop. My body felt cold, wet, and achy. As if I had just been beaten up by a snowman. We all sank into chairs, except for Aunt Erma, who went to turn up the heat and bring down dry socks for everyone. Mitzy followed her downstairs, eager to cheer up the exhausted crowd with her wagging tail.

Henry put his arm on my shoulder. "I hate to leave you right now, but I'm supposed to help the residents decorate for Christmas, and I have to stop at home to let Willy out first."

"Go, go," Aunt Erma said. "We're fine here." I tried to force a smile to show him, yes, of course we were fine. Aunt Erma said it, so it must be true.

He studied my face for a second and hesitated as though he knew what I was feeling. "I'll check in with you later," he said, giving my shoulder a squeeze.

He left and we all sat in silence for a minute. Aunt Erma's eyes had drifted closed. Then they snapped open.

"Aren't you supposed to go help him?" she asked.

"Well, yes, but—" I began.

"But nothing," she said. "Everything is just fine here. You go and help string up those lights."

I felt torn. I loved decorating for Christmas, and I loved the enthusiasm and complete lack of boundaries that most people in the nursing home had, but there was anxiety in the pit of my stomach at the thought of leaving Aunt Erma alone. It was dangerous. Even I knew it was bad that the IMPs had hit right here in town.

"You go. You can all go," Aunt Erma insisted. "I've got my guard dog." Right on cue, Mitzy let out a cheerful yip. "I'm ready to have a quiet night in and try out some new pie recipes."

"Okay," I said hesitantly. "I'll just go upstairs and change."

"I can walk you there," Mr. Barnes offered.

"I'll be fine," I said, trying to adopt Aunt Erma's bravado. "It's, like, a three-block walk. I'll be there in no time."

"Okay," he said, still looking a little unsure, but he left and the rest of the Morning Pie Crew reluctantly stood.

"Are you sure you don't want me to stay?" Flora asked. Aunt Erma turned her down, but that didn't stop her from asking three more times before Aunt Erma ushered her to the door.

I went upstairs to put on a drier outfit. I settled on a bright red tunic with black leggings. It was both Christmassy and allowed me to move in case I needed to tackle any other rogue snowmen.

122

"Keep an eye on Aunt Erma," I told Mitzy. She wagged her tail at me.

"Bye, Aunt Erma," I called as I headed towards the back door. She appeared from the front of the shop. "I'll be back soon," I told her.

"Pish posh." She dismissed me with a wave. "You stay out as long as you want. You kids have fun with all those old fogies." I gave her a hug and was out the door. I kept my eyes peeled for any stray snowmen who might roll into my path and attack at any moment.

Chapter 8

Dear Elodie,

I have a co-worker in the cubicle next to mine who hums all day long! I've tried to clear my throat loudly, hoping he'll get the message, but he just keeps humming the most annoying songs. How do I get him to stop?

Sincerely,
Hassled by Humming

Dear Hassled by Humming,

Dare I suggest that you talk to your co-worker and ask him to stop?

Ask and I'll Answer,

Elodie

Despite my bravado when talking to Mr. Barnes, it was the longest three-block walk I'd ever taken. Even the sound of the wind rustling through the trees was enough to make the hair on my arms stand at attention. The streets were deserted after the earlier fiasco, which only added to my uneasiness.

So when my phone rang, I yelped and then tried to cover it with a cough, even though no one was around to hear me. It wasn't a number I recognized. I slid the button and answered.

"Susie Daniels?" a gruff voice asked.

"This is she," I said cautiously. I kicked myself for answering what sounded as if it was going to be a sales call.

"This is Buster Hopkins from Top-Notch Construction." I stood up a little straighter. He was one of the bigwigs in the construction scene in the city. "I hear you left Hal's."

That was one way of putting it. Hal had fired me when I took some time off to come help Aunt Erma at the pie shop.

"I want to offer you a job," he said. "I've seen some of your work, and I really admire your craftsmanship." He told me what my starting salary would be, and my mouth fell open. "Everyone I've talked to has great things to say about you. Well, everyone except Hal, but he's a bitter old fusspot, isn't he? So what do you say?"

"Can I think about it?" I asked. I was standing outside the nursing home now. I traced the gold letters on the sign out front that read "Enchanted Woods", briefly forgetting my fear of rogue snowmen.

"Sure, we'll talk soon," he said and hung up.

As I walked towards the door, I shivered with excitement and anxiety. This job offer was a big deal, but was I ready to leave the life I had just started in Hocus Hills?

All of my concerns melted away, though, the moment I stepped inside. The warmth washed over me. I could hear voices singing "Rockin' Around the Christmas Tree" and by the time I got to the dining room, the smell of food had brought my blood pressure down to a reasonable level and reminded me how incredibly hungry I was.

I peeked through the door. Henry was playing the piano and everyone was singing. I could hear his smooth voice and felt a rush of excitement. My mind wandered back to our kiss, and I watched his fingers dance over the keys. I flushed and shook my head. Three couples were dancing around the Christmas tree. I held my breath as Mrs. Portman dipped Mrs. Bishop, but, despite their frail appearance, they performed the maneuver flawlessly.

"Susie, come and dance," Henry called out over the noise. Frank, a man whose large glasses accentuated his twinkling blue eyes, stretched his hand out towards me. I took it, and he spun me around while singing every word. The song ended, and he gave me a gentlemanly bow as I thanked him for the dance.

"Looks like you guys waited for me to get started on the decorating," I said, looking at all the unopened boxes on the floor around the room.

Henry shrugged. "We may have gotten a little distracted."

"Last year it took us three weeks to get the Christmas

decorations up because we kept getting distracted with sing-a-longs." Frank grinned.

"And dance-alongs," Claire Sprinkles added, approaching us with a little sashay.

"Maybe we can get one box done today," I said, going to the nearest box and opening it. It was full of a tangle of Christmas lights. "Who put these away?" I asked, pulling out the giant mess. "Is there magic to untangle these?"

They laughed. "No, we usually let the newest member of the Christmas decorating team take care of that," someone said.

"So it's my job, huh?" I said. I couldn't even see an end. "I think it looks good like this." I brought it over to an outlet and plugged it in. The lights were almost blinding, but beautiful. I decided it was probably too much of a fire hazard to leave like that. "I'll work on this." I sat on the floor with the ball in my lap. I was eager to take a job that didn't include hanging shiny Christmas baubles. I didn't want to risk seeing a face other than my own peering back at me. I shivered.

"Are you cold?" Henry asked, coming up behind me.

I looked at him incredulously. "Is it possible to be cold in this place?" I asked. They kept it so warm in here, I often fantasized about jumping in the snow to make snow angels when I stayed here for longer than ten minutes. "It's nothing," I said, forcing a smile. When he looked at me harder with his intense gaze, the one I was learning to both love and hate, I said, "I'll tell you more later."

"Here." He set down a plate piled with fluffy mashed potatoes. "I thought you might be hungry."

I threw my arms around him. "Thank you."

He looked a little taken aback. "You're welcome." He squeezed me tightly.

"Now, that's how you know a couple is going to last," Frank said from his perch by the dessert table. "They show their appreciation for the small things."

I smiled at him, but felt knots in my stomach.

"I can help you with this," Henry said, pointing to the giant mess.

"No, this is all mine. I want all the glory when it's all done," I said. I had finally found an end and began to unwind it through the mess. "I do, however, want to be here when the Christmas lights are put away this year. I will carefully wind them up," I said.

"I *was* careful when I put them away last year," Claire Sprinkles spoke up indignantly.

"You weren't careful," Bernie said. "You drank a gallon of spiked eggnog and then wound them around your body and sang about being the light of our lives."

She paused for a second, not looking the slightest bit sheepish. "Oh yeah, that's right." Then she burst into laughter. "Maybe you'd better come back and put them away. I still really love eggnog."

I tried to focus on the project in front of me, but it was wonderfully distracting to be among this much positive energy. People were hanging Christmas decorations on the tree, pulling them out of boxes and laughing with stories about who bought them and what they represented.

Claire Sprinkles told a wildly inappropriate story about the "special fella" who bought her the ornament shaped like a bottle of champagne. I hummed along to the Christmas music playing in the background, and every now and then Henry would stop by to see how it was going. I was making headway, but it was a slow process. He was generally too busy trying to keep Frank from climbing up on a chair to put the ornaments on top of the tree.

"No, Frank," he would call. "You can reach the top of the tree from the ground." He would rush over and grab him just as he was about to make the step up onto the chair. Apparently Frank had fallen off a chair last year and broken a hip. Climbing chairs was the least of his daring adventures though. Henry said sometimes he went out at night, found a sled, and tried to get up on the roof to slide off it.

"He used to be a bobsledder. He made it to some big international competitions too," Henry said, and told me he was arranging a special bobsled experience for Frank this winter. He'd bought a used bobsled and had made plans to build a track out of snow on the hill at the edge of town.

"I just hope he makes it until that day," Henry said, rushing off to stop him from using the sofa as a trampoline to jump to the tree with an ornament in his hand.

I texted Aunt Erma to make sure she was okay. She responded, "Everything's peachy here, including the pie," and sent a picture of a peach pie. She told me she wanted to use some of the peaches she had canned last summer to bring a bit of warmth to this freezing weather. A minute later, another text came in. "Now stop bothering me and drink some eggnog." I smiled.

Two hours later, and I had successfully untangled the mess of lights. The whole room applauded and then helped me hang them. They filled the room with a colorful warm glow, and for the first time this year I felt giddy for the upcoming holidays. I briefly wondered what I could get Henry. Clearly Henry was a very thoughtful gift-giver. Just look at what he was going to do for Mr. Labelle. I was generally the "buy him a sweater" type, but clearly I was going to have to step up my game now.

"I should probably get back to Aunt Erma now," I said after we'd all enjoyed mugs of hot chocolate and a few more Christmas songs had been sung.

"I'll walk you out in just a second," Henry said. Then he began singing, "Silent Night". The whole room chimed in, and Henry used the opportunity to follow me out to the front of the nursing home.

"Aren't you worried about leaving them alone right now? Frank keeps eyeing that sofa," I said.

"They'll go to sleep as soon as they sing this song," he said. "It works every time." Then he yawned. "I might go to sleep after this song too."

We got to the front door and Henry leaned down to give me a kiss. I felt the tingling in my fingertips as I always did.

Giant snowflakes were falling gently from the sky as I jogged back to the pie shop – just because it was cold, I told my ego, not because I was afraid anymore. I ran down the alley and let myself in the back door because I didn't want to see a reflection in the windows at the front of the shop. I had myself so worked up by the time I got there that I was pretty sure I would see Brenda's face even if she wasn't there.

I flew through the door and slammed it behind me, locking it quickly as though that could keep the bad magic out. I closed my eyes and took a deep breath, letting the warmth at the back of the kitchen wash over me.

My eyes flew open when I heard a clatter right in front of me. Aunt Erma was in the kitchen pulling things out of the cupboard and throwing them on the kitchen island. She didn't even look over at me.

"Hi, Aunt Erma," I said. She pulled out a handful of mixing spoons from a drawer and set them on the counter. "Did everything go okay while I was gone?" She walked around the island, grabbed a pie tin, and wandered back to the cupboard to put it away. "Aunt Erma," I said again. She still didn't even look my way. She just walked over to the handful of spoons and put them back in the drawer.

"Is everything okay?" I asked louder, even though she wasn't that far away from me. She took the bottle of soap that was by the sink and set it on her desk at the back of the kitchen. As she turned and headed for the pantry, I grabbed her arm. Something was definitely off about the way she squinted at me.

"I'm going to call 911," I said.

"Sometimes I hide the last slice of blueberry pie and tell customers we're sold out, so I can eat it," she announced, and then wrenched her arm out of my grip as she headed back towards the pantry. This didn't seem like a medical emergency anymore. This seemed like magic.

Chapter 9

Dear Elodie,

I married a woman who claimed to be a perpetual truth-teller. I admired her for that, and it was even one of the qualities that attracted me to her. She didn't pull any punches, and I always knew what she was thinking. In the last couple years, it's gotten out of control. She'll tell strangers on the street that their baby is ugly. She told my mother her family famous vegetable stew was inedible. She's told countless friends that we don't want to get together with them because they are too boring. I'm losing friends and family and becoming increasingly resentful toward my wife. I've tried to show my disapproval, but nothing seems to work. What can I do?

Sincerely,
Truthfully Terrible

Dear Truthfully Terrible,

It sounds like she's hiding behind a mask of honesty as she slings insults. You say that you've tried to show your disapproval. Does that include having a serious conversation with your wife? Sometimes people like to say shocking things just to see a reaction. Find out what your wife's reasons are for saying these things when you talk to her. Just be prepared for her "honest" response.

Ask and I'll Answer,

Elodie

"Was anyone here?" I asked Aunt Erma. She began to hum, "Let it Snow".

I pulled out my phone and called Flora first, because she was the closest. Then I called Violet and my mother. Flora was at the door before I even finished the conversation with my mother. Aunt Erma was still wandering around the kitchen moving things in and out of cupboards and drawers. I had a feeling we wouldn't be able to find anything by the time she was done undoing her very carefully organized system.

Flora stood and observed for a minute. Then she slowly approached Aunt Erma as though she was afraid she would spook her. She spoke some words I couldn't understand. I assumed she was trying a spell. Aunt Erma paused for a minute and then kept puttering around. Flora hurried around the island so that she was standing in front of her again and murmured some more words. I stood in the corner of the kitchen feeling helpless and guilty. I shouldn't have left her alone. I grabbed a scrub brush from the sink and pushed it down on the counter until all the bristles bowed out.

"I don't care for that new haircut," Aunt Erma said before brushing past Flora to open the drawer with all the measuring cups. She grabbed one pile of red measuring cups and one pile of green and mixed them up, stacking them so they alternated colors.

My mom rushed in a few minutes later. She was wearing her sleek black coat over her yellow floral nightgown. Behind her, the snow fell off her in a trail of flakes.

"What is it?" she asked. "Erma, what's wrong?"

Aunt Erma handed my mom a handful of forks and said, "You have bony elbows." My mother looked at me wide-eyed, and I shrugged.

"She was like this when I came home," I said. I wanted to cry, but instead I focused on a screw that was coming loose on the side of the desk. I should really fix that.

"Do you have any idea what it is?" my mother asked Flora.

"It looks like a truth spell gone wrong," Flora said. "I think we can guess who the culprits are."

My mother and Flora were talking at the other end of the kitchen, and I went over to Aunt Erma where she was crouched down pulling everything out from under the sink. I bent down next to her and took out a bottle of cleaner.

"Aunt Erma, did you tell them anything?" I asked in a low voice, thinking of the magic tree.

"Yes." Aunt Erma nodded solemnly. Her earnest eyes stared into mine for a moment. "I told them that I love pickles." I let out the breath I was holding. I stood up and took a few steps back to lean against the kitchen island.

Violet arrived. Despite the late hour, she was still in a navy business suit with her hair slicked back into a bun.

It felt as if we were all getting together far too often to do things other than celebrate Christmas. She went straight to Aunt Erma without saying a word. She murmured some words, but they didn't seem to have any more effect than Flora's did.

"Why is she rearranging the kitchen?" I asked. We all watched Aunt Erma cross the kitchen with a stack of plates.

"She's very strong," Violet said. "Most people on the receiving end of this spell would spill every secret they ever had. She's fighting the magic."

"Why didn't they take her with them?" I asked.

"They probably couldn't. Not with the protection spells she has on this place," Violet said. "I honestly don't know how they got to her at all. I can't seem to undo whatever spell they used."

"Fairy dust," my mother cried out, making me jump so high I knocked the handful of forks off the counter.

Everyone turned towards her, except Aunt Erma, who pulled a handful of flour out of a bag. My mother was digging in her purse without further explanation. She produced a bottle of sparkling dust. It was a small bottle very similar to the one I had used a few weeks ago to turn Aunt Erma back into a human after being a cat. I couldn't believe she had fairy dust. I thought she was against most of the magic stuff.

"Here." She waved it around wildly.

"That might work," Flora said cautiously.

"Do you know the right spell," Violet asked.

My mother glared at her, and Violet held her hands up in mock surrender. I was just glad I wasn't on the receiving end of that look.

My mother walked closer to Aunt Erma. "Erma," she said. "Erma?"

Aunt Erma tilted her head to the side. "I put Susie's Christmas present under my bed," she said.

My mother poured a bit of the fairy dust onto the palm of her hand. Just as she was about to sprinkle it over Aunt Erma's head, Aunt Erma backed away and headed for the pantry.

"I'm going to need some help here," my mother said. We all moved in to help keep Aunt Erma still. She looked at me. I tried to smile, but it felt shaky.

"Keep the dog from the tree," she said to me.

Everyone turned towards me. "What does that mean?" Violet asked.

I shrugged because I really didn't know. I assumed she was talking about her super-secret magic tree, but I didn't know what the dog stuff was about. Mitzy was upstairs. Maybe she was trying to tell me she needed the magic from the tree.

My mother was saying the spell and sprinkling the dust.

After she was done, Aunt Erma looked at her for a minute. We all stood back and held our breath.

"I took your Sally Sparkles doll when we were kids," Aunt Erma said to my mom. Then she scooted past Violet and to the pantry.

"I knew it was you," my mother muttered.

"What about the spices?" I asked.

"We could try them," Flora said, "but I'm not sure how much they would do since all the other magic isn't working."

I went to the fridge and pulled out every kind of pie we had in there. I didn't bother with slicing, I just stuck a fork in each one and scooped out a bite. The first one was apple. I held the bite in front of Aunt Erma's mouth, but she sidestepped it. I swirled it through the air like an airplane. I didn't realize how crazy I looked until I saw the expressions on everyone's face around me.

"Aunt Erma, please take a bite," I tried instead.

"Okay," she said, and took the bite in her mouth. I did that with the remaining pies. At the end, she didn't seem any better.

"What do we do now?" I asked. I assumed someone else had another plan, but everyone exchanged hopeless glances.

"I'll go do some more research. If I can figure out exactly what spell was used and how it went wrong, then maybe we can undo it," Violet said.

"Maybe it will wear off soon too," I suggested. All of

Aunt Erma's spices only worked for short periods of time. I assumed this would be temporary too.

"Yeah, maybe," Flora said in a voice that adults used when they told children that, "yeah, maybe," Santa would show up for dinner.

Violet and Flora left, and my mother and I brought Aunt Erma upstairs. Mitzy was waiting by the door as usual. She ran towards Aunt Erma then stopped in her tracks and backed away.

"It's okay, Mitzy," I said, but she just whined.

"Come on, Erma. Let's watch some television," my mom said. We led Aunt Erma over to the sofa, which doubled as my bed. She sat down and stared at the blank screen. I turned it on and flipped through the channels until I found a mindless sitcom. I didn't think we needed a crime drama or something as horrific as the news on a night like tonight.

Mitzy walked in circles around the room, whining. Her tail was tucked between her legs.

"You should take Mitzy on a walk," my mother said. "I'll stay here with Erma."

I agreed, grabbing my coat and Mitzy's leash. Usually that was enough to initiate an enthusiastic response, but Mitzy just kept circling.

"Do you want to go on a walk?" I used my high-pitched dog voice, but even that didn't make her dance around my feet like she usually did. Finally, I went over to her and clipped the leash to her collar and led her out the door.

She followed slowly with her head down. It's okay, Mitz," I told her softly on our way down the stairs.

The snow was still falling in fluffy flakes as we walked through the streets of the town. I wished I could enjoy the beautiful snow and sparkling Christmas lights, but thoughts swirled around in my mind and my head felt as if it were going to explode from the building panic. What if we never broke the spell? What if the IMPs discovered the magic tree? Had Aunt Erma given them any clues? Could the tree break the spell? How could I find the tree again? If Aunt Erma thought that I could just go out and find it again after seeing it once, she vastly overestimated my memory, but I vowed to try anyway.

Mitzy walked slowly alongside me. She didn't stop to sniff every light pole and tree as she usually did, which made me feel more unsettled. Of all the times I had wanted her to behave, now I wanted her to act like her normal nutty self. I took her all the way around the square. I was hoping she would perk up, and I wanted to survey the scene of the earlier insanity. Someone had cleaned up quite well. All of the props were gone and the snow had been smoothed out so no one could tell it had been the site of a major snowman massacre. The Christmas lights twinkled brightly, happy to keep the secret. The only evidence left from the contest was a carrot stuck way up in a pine tree. We turned the last corner of the square and were going to head back to the pie shop, when Mitzy made an abrupt turn down a side street.

"No, Mitzy, this way," I said. I gently tugged at her leash, but she stood at attention and pointed her paw down the road. That was another new behavior. I weighed my options and followed her. It occurred to me that she was under some sort of spell too and that I was being led into a trap. "Mitzy, where are you taking me?" I asked. I decided a couple weeks ago that talking to dogs was, in fact, acceptable behavior. Especially when the dog seemed to understand every word that you said.

She pulled at the leash again and I followed. We approached Mr. Barnes's yoga studio, and I heard a loud clatter come from inside. I hurried towards the front door. I hesitated when I heard the sound of breaking glass but Mitzy pulled harder at her leash. She began to growl, and I tried to shush her. What should I do? Call Violet? Go inside and see what was happening? I debated.

"You thieving son of a ..." I heard Mr. Barnes's voice inside. The time for debating was over. Mitzy and I rushed through the front door of the yoga studio. There were only a few candles lit, providing a flickering light. I felt the walls, trying to find a light switch, but I couldn't find one.

"Mr. Barnes, are you okay?" I called. There was another crash. Mitzy tugged at her leash, growling and barking with the ferocity of a much bigger dog. "Mr. Barnes?" I called again. I felt something brush past me, and I tried to grab it. My fingers caught a corner of cloth, and I held on tightly, but the cloth quickly went limp. Light filled the shop, and I had to squint against the brightness to see. Mr.

Barnes stood at the corner of the room by a light switch. He had his hands on his knees, and he was breathing hard. I looked down at my hands. I was clutching a gray jacket. Mitzy had her teeth sunk into the other corner of the fabric. She had a look of determination in her eyes, but when she saw there was no one wearing it anymore, she let it go. I recognized the jacket. It was Stan's. I let it slide out of my fingers and into a pile on the ground.

"What happened?" I asked. My heart was still racing.

"Someone was in here." Mr. Barnes paused to take a deep, cleansing yoga breath. "They stole from me." He waved his arm around as though he was going to say more, but he didn't.

"I think it was Stan." I pointed to the jacket. "I'll call Violet." I had her on speed dial now. Violet appeared quickly, still in her business suit. I wondered if she had any lounge clothes. I imagined her in flannel business suit pajamas.

"I went to the diner to grab a bite to eat," Mr. Barnes began. "When I came back I lit a few candles." He was pacing across the studio now. "Why didn't I turn on the lights? I was trying to relax." He answered his own question as he rubbed his hands through his hair.

"What happened next?" Violet prompted.

"I just started doing my nightly yoga exercises when I heard something and headed toward the light switch. That's when someone bumped into me." He walked over to Stan's jacket and kicked it across the floor.

Mr. Barnes and Violet talked about the spells that were thrown back and forth during the fight, most of which I hadn't heard of.

"He took my carving." Mr. Barnes pointed to a shelf on the wall where he'd had a carving of a gnome doing the splits. I had noticed it during the few yoga classes I had taken. Mr. Barnes said it was supposed to provide inspiration, but I thought the smiling gnome mocked my lack of flexibility every time I tried to touch my toes.

"Why would he do that?" I asked. It seemed like a lot of trouble to go to for a gnome.

"Erma gave it to me," he said.

"It had some of her magic in it," Violet explained when she saw I still didn't understand. "She might have let something slip when under the spell that led them here."

"She gave it to me to protect my studio and promote calm within these walls." He was still looking at the empty shelf. My eyes widened as I wondered if it was carved out of wood from the magic tree. Could they locate the tree by using the gnome? I clamped my mouth shut to keep myself from asking my questions out loud.

"We'll find it." Violet put her hand on Mr. Barnes's shoulder in a rare display of affection. "I'll let you know when I know something." And with that, she was out the door.

I left a few minutes later, after making sure that Mr. Barnes was all right. "I'm fine. It's nothing a little herbal tea won't fix," he said.

When I stepped outside, the snow was deep with the flakes falling so fast and thick, I could barely see Mitzy in front of me. I knew I would never be able to make it to the magic tree in these conditions. I would have to try tomorrow.

Or maybe Aunt Erma would be better by tomorrow and I wouldn't need to go, I thought hopefully.

Chapter 10

Dear Elodie,

Last Christmas, my mother gave me a necklace that had belonged to her mother and her mother's mother, all the way back to my great-great-great-grandmother. It was a beautiful gold pendant with stars and a tree engraved on it. I was thrilled when I received this family heirloom. My mother always said I couldn't be trusted with nice things, and when she presented the gift, she warned me to be very careful with it because, if I lost it, the ghost of my great-great-great-grandmother would come back and curse me.

You can probably see where this is going. I wore it to an event the other night because it went so perfectly with my outfit and I'm a firm believer in not letting things just sit in a drawer and collect dust. I was on my way home when I realized it wasn't around my neck anymore. I looked everywhere in the car and even went back to the venue and searched on my hands and knees. The staff there tried to help, but no one found it.

Now I'm not sleeping and feel sick with worry. Worry over telling my mom. Worry that my great-great-great-grandmother will come back and curse me, and worry that I really can't be trusted with nice things.

Do you know any tricks for locating something that's lost? How do I get over this guilt and get on with my life?
Sincerely,
Lost and Never Found

Dear Lost and Never Found,

The first thing you have to do is remind yourself that accidents happen. Heirlooms can be wonderful ways to connect generations, but they can also be a burden when people end up with things they're so stressed out about losing that they never use them.

The second thing you should do is explain to your mother what happened, and brace for what might be a less than ideal reaction. It sounds like the worry over telling her is eating you up, and you should just get it over with.

The third thing you should do is try social media. If you have a picture of the pendant, post it on social media, specifically engaging with people who were at the event with you. Maybe someone picked it up without realizing the significance of it.

Maybe you and your mother could go out together and look for something that could be the new family heirloom. Every heirloom has to begin somewhere.

A Slice of Christmas Magic

*As for your great-great-great-grandmother, I hope
she would understand. If nothing else, maybe she'll curse
the person who took the pendant instead of cursing
you.*

Ask and I'll Answer,

Elodie

Early the next morning, I held my breath as I slowly
pushed the blanket off and carefully put my foot on
the floor. My mother had stayed over to help me keep an
eye on Aunt Erma and she was now curled up asleep on
the purple chair next to me. I had begged her to sleep on
the sofa, saying I would sleep in the chair, but she'd refused,
which made things difficult.

I'd figured she would sleep more soundly on the sofa,
but also that I would have a slightly better chance of
sneaking out in the morning to go to the tree as my mother
was a very light sleeper. The kind of person you'd want
around if you were sleeping in a cave wary of a bear attack,
but not the kind of person you'd want around if you were
trying to sneak out. I had tried to sneak out a few times
in high school when I was going through my wild-child
phase, but I wouldn't even get to the front door before my
mom was yelling, "Susanna Penelope Maxine Bennett
Daniels, where in the world do you think you're going at
this hour?" If I'd been a more daring teenager, I would
have used the time she spent saying all five of my names
to make a run for it.

149

I crept over to the window. Mitzy stirred in Aunt Erma's room. Don't ruin this for me, dog, I thought. As though she could hear my thoughts, she settled back in.

I pulled back the edge of the curtain. The snow had stopped, and there was just the faintest light in the sky. Good. I should have time to find the tree and get back before everyone woke up.

I was tiptoeing to the door when the phone rang. My mother leapt out of the chair.

"What's wrong?" she asked. Her hair stuck straight out on one side of her head and her eyes were wild with panic.

"It's the phone. I've got it," I said. The whole apartment was awake now. I cursed whoever was calling as I hurried over to answer it.

Flora was on the other end of the line. "Violet called. She wants you and Lena and I to go check out Lily Ridge," she said. Lily Ridge was another nearby town. "It looks like the IMPs have struck again."

"Already?" I groaned. This was a lot to take before I had my coffee.

"Can you be ready in five minutes?" she asked.

"Do you guys really need me?" I asked. I was still hoping to go find the magic tree.

"Violet thinks we might need your magic, and she doesn't think they realize how bad Erma is. Mr. Barnes will help your mother at the pie shop," she said. "Bring some of the spices. See you in five."

I explained the situation to my mother as I threw on some jeans, a hooded sweatshirt, and my jacket. I quickly splashed some water on my face and pulled my mess of hair back into a low ponytail before shoving a knit hat on my head. Downstairs in the kitchen, I opened the latch on the sparkly wooden box with the swirly designs where Aunt Erma kept her spices, and I grabbed a few bottles. When I got outside, Flora was already warming up her SUV. I had been surprised when I first found out Flora drove such a big vehicle.

"Books are heavy and take up a lot of space and sometimes I have to transport a lot of them," she'd explained. "And I wouldn't be able to do that if I drove a teensy little car like yours."

Lena came flying out of the front of the hardware store. She had just thrown boots and a coat over her red flannel pajamas. She skidded to a stop by the SUV before jumping in. "What is with these people?" she asked breathlessly. "Can't they take a few days off so we can enjoy the holiday season?"

"How could they not know how bad Aunt Erma is?" I asked. "They did this to her."

"They probably think the effects were just temporary. And if they do figure out that she's as bad as she is, they might try something bigger," Flora explained.

I thought about the tree and how it might fix everything. I desperately wanted to tell Flora and Lena about it, so they could help me, but I had made a promise to Aunt

Erma. I knew she wouldn't understand if I broke her trust. Even in a dire situation like this.

I sighed and leaned back in the seat. Warm air was blowing out of the vents, and my eyelids felt heavy. Lena and Flora were talking strategy. I shook my head a little to wake up.

Apparently, the security cameras showed the residents of Lily Ridge gathering for a large cookie-baking day.

"That doesn't sound any stranger than having a snowman-building contest," I said.

"It is when it happens at four in the morning," Lena said.

"Good point."

"Their magic could be stronger too, since they took that carving from Mr. Barnes's studio," Lena warned. They thought Aunt Erma had bought the magic wooden carving during one of her grand traveling adventures.

"Violet is worried that they've made more progress with their altered spices, and they want to do a widespread test of the effects, so they're doing it with cookies," Flora said.

"Oh, for Christmas' sake, what is their obsession with cookies?" Lena said.

We had a basic plan in place by the time Flora was pulling into a parking lot near the local Lily Ridge grocery store. I was going to begin sprinkling Aunt Erma's original spices in the cookie dough. The magic in our spices was supposed to counteract the magic in the altered spices. Flora and Lena were supposed to start bagging the cookies that they'd already baked so we could get rid of them.

It was pretty easy to track down where everyone was. We just followed the smell of cookies. After all the drama with Alice last month, the thought of cookies still made me shudder, but they sure did smell good. My heart wasn't beating quite as fast as it would have a week ago. This time I felt ready for battle. My emotional armor was getting thicker with each magical encounter.

I clutched the bottles of spices tightly in my hands as we walked towards the door of the bakery. It was a white stucco building. A large dark blue sign hung over the door. The words "Eastside Bakery" were painted in bold white letters. The door was propped open, but when we stepped inside, it was warm even on this frigid morning.

This scene was different than the chaos at the church where they were knitting the mitten. This time all of the people were focused and intense. They were working quickly and efficiently. That couldn't be good. They were definitely improving their spells.

We got to work. Flora fluffed up a couple of garbage bags, and she and Lena grabbed cookie sheets and dumped them into their bags. I was a little jealous that they had the fun job. After Alice, I felt as if it would be satisfying to dump a bunch of cookies into the garbage.

I went to the giant mixer on the side of the kitchen that was mixing up a large batch of light brown dough. I sprinkled a healthy amount of Aunt Erma's spice number five in it. I carefully approached a man wearing a chef's hat, who was rolling out a large sheet of dough. There were two men and a woman next to him. They were wearing their pajamas and cutting out shapes with cookie cutters. They all gazed at their work intently, pressing their cookie cutters down in quick systematic movements. I slowly reached in front of them to sprinkle spice on the dough they were working with.

"You're not supposed to be here." The man rolling the dough glared at me sharply. He had curly reddish-brown hair and a goatee. He was probably a lovely person when he wasn't under a spell. I glanced at Lena. Was this a normal part of the spell? Lena's pinched eyebrows clued me in that it wasn't.

I felt a layer of my confidence dissolve.

"This must be a new addition to the spell," she said, just as a giant wad of cookie dough hit me in the face. Before I had time to see where it came from, the cookie dough was flying at me fast and furious from every direction. So far Lena and Flora had gone undetected. Voices kept yelling, "You're not supposed to be here." I threw another dash of the spice on the cut-outs on the table and dodged the flying dough when I could. I added a little spice to the open bag of flour for good measure and then ran out the front door. And straight into Josh.

"Your aunt told me you were here," he said.

Darn truth spell.

"This isn't a great time," I said, wiping a giant glob of cookie dough out of my hair. I glanced behind me. No one had followed me out.

He surveyed me as though realizing for the first time that something was off. "What's going on here?"

"Nothing, just a food fight," I said with a nervous chuckle, and I led him away from the scene in case anyone decided to check to make sure I was gone. We went around the corner, and I saw he had parked his dark blue truck next to Flora's yellow SUV. Once we were a safe distance away, I said, "So what's up?"

"I can't have a serious conversation with you when you're covered in ... What are you covered in?" he asked.

"Cookie dough." I felt a blob slide down my back and shifted uncomfortably. "It's part of this small-town Christmas scavenger hunt." I waved it off as though any further explanation would bore him. "How's the job going?"

"Good," he said. "They've changed all the switch plate covers six times, but hopefully this time they'll stick."

Lena and Flora rounded the corner, each dragging four bags of cookies.

"Start the car," Lena yelled. I didn't have the keys for the SUV, but I ran to help them. Josh was right beside me and grabbed three of the bags. People poured out of the bakery, running towards us. The bags wouldn't all fit in Flora's car, so we threw some in the back of Josh's truck. Somehow in the chaos, Lena ended up in Josh's truck, and Flora and I were in the SUV. We all sped off seconds before the mob reached us. I felt exhilarated by our escape and bounced up and down in my seat.

I hoped Lena would be able to explain this all to Josh.

I didn't envy her being in that position, but she was a smooth-talker.

During the drive, I apologized several times to Flora for getting cookie dough all over her car seat. She assured me she could clean it off in no time. When we got back to Hocus Hills we pulled the cars around behind the pie shop so we could dispose of the bags of cookies in the dumpster. Aunt Erma must have heard the commotion because she stuck her head out.

"Hi, Aunt Erma," I said, hoping beyond hope that she would answer me normally.

"Sometimes I steal rolls of toilet paper from restaurants," she said.

"Thanks for sharing." I let out a disappointed laugh. Lena and Flora joined in, glancing uneasily at Josh. We threw the bags in the dumpster. Aunt Erma sized Josh up.

"You don't belong in this world. You're not safe here," she said. He raised his eyebrows and looked at me.

Flora quickly ushered Aunt Erma back inside. I grabbed Josh by the corner of his sweatshirt and led him back towards his truck.

"She's been really stressed out," I said. "I don't think she's sleeping very well." He politely accepted this explanation. "Just a sec," I said, and I jogged over to Lena. She was just about to go inside too.

"Hey, I have something I have to go take care of," I said in a low voice, eyeing Josh meaningfully.

"Say no more." She nodded knowingly. "We have things under control here." She disappeared inside.

I went back over to Josh. "It seems like you're busy. Maybe we can talk another time," he said.

"Yeah, we'll talk soon," I said. I was about to give him a hug when I realized I was still covered in cookie dough. So I just waved instead. I took this opportunity to run to my car. I was going to find the magic tree.

I shook off as much cookie dough as I could. A lot of it had dried and fell off in sugary crumbs. I turned my coat inside out so I wouldn't get the seat too dirty – my poor car had been through enough in its long lifetime – but a little dough still smeared across the seat as I slid in. I was trying to keep a low profile as I drove through town, so I crouched down as though that would keep people from recognizing me. As if the loud mufflerless red car certainly wouldn't tip them off.

I merged onto the highway and tried to visualize which exit Aunt Erma had taken. I glanced in my rear-view mirror and noticed a big dark green car behind me. It had been behind me for a while. Was I being paranoid? This kind of thing only happened on television. Then again, the people on television who were being followed usually dismissed the danger because they told themselves that this kind of thing only happened on television. Then something unspeakable happened to them. I switched lanes, keeping an eye on the green car in my rear-view mirror. It didn't switch lanes. I let out a sigh of relief and turned my attention back to finding the tree.

This exit looked familiar. I pulled off and drove until I found a dirt road. Had there been a rock on the corner last time? I didn't remember a rock.

I turned around and tried a different road and then a different one, but I couldn't find the spot. I got out of the car a couple times to wander through the woods. I even tried calling to the tree. I felt a little silly calling to the tree as though it were a dog, but this was a desperate time. I thought the tree would give me something, somehow show me where it was hiding. I listened in the wind for the delicate sound of the baubles clinking together, but nothing.

I was afraid to wander too far away from the car because the last thing I needed was to get lost in the woods. I never watched those survival shows closely enough, and I didn't know how to do things like start a fire or find clean water and food. Lena told me once that there was a spell to start fires, but Aunt Erma refused to teach it to me. Probably because of the one time, okay *two* times, I'd almost burned down the pie shop. These things could happen to anyone.

I wearily drove back to the pie shop, my stomach swirling with the anxiety of failure.

Chapter 11

Dear Elodie,

Three years ago, I lost my husband in a car accident. I miss him every day, and it's a thousand times worse at the holidays. I have a friend who regularly texts me pictures of her and her husband doing different things, especially around the holidays. Her and her husband with Santa, her and her husband on a sleigh ride, her and her husband skiing. Every picture she sends crushes my spirit a little more, and I get stuck dwelling on how I can't do those things with my husband.

I don't think she knows what her pictures are doing to me, but I don't know how to stop her from sending them to me without seeming rude and bitter.

For the past two years, every time we're together, she tells me about the latest guy she's met that she wants to set me up with. I try to tell her I'm not ready, but she just brushes it off, saying I don't know what's good for me.

We've been friends for a long time. She was really

there for me after my husband died. I still miss my husband, and I'm not ready to meet someone new yet.

How do I handle this situation? Do I just need to toughen up?

Sincerely,
Single and Not Ready to Mingle

Dear Single and Not Ready to Mingle,

It sounds like your friend's heart might be in the right place, but her actions definitely leave a little to be desired. You said she's a good friend. She probably sees your unhappiness and is trying to fix it. That is certainly easier said than done. Try to sit down with your friend, and have a frank conversation about how her actions are affecting you. Tell her that you're very happy for her, but you're still struggling, and her pictures and constant matchmaking attempts aren't helping. You will find someone if and when you're ready to.

You asked if you need to toughen up. The answer is no. Your grief isn't on anyone else's schedule. However, if you're feeling like the weight of this all is too heavy, you should really seek counseling. A counselor might help you deal with your grief, especially during the holidays. There are also a lot of support groups out there with people who are feeling the same way you are.

Ask and I'll Answer,

Elodie

Mr. Barnes was the first of the Morning Pie Crew through the door the next day. The morning rush had come and gone, people rushing in to pick up their pies for whatever holiday event they had going on that day, and I had just finished wiping off the front tables.

Aunt Erma was still spilling all of her secrets, but at least her frantic rearranging had stopped. We had been telling people that she had the flu so word wouldn't get out that she was under a bad spell. I think people were buying it too. Three people had brought in soup for her and another four had brought in their "special elixirs".

We had managed to focus Aunt Erma on the great task of organizing photos for photo albums. She had boxes and boxes of pictures in her closet. A couple weeks ago she had gone digging in her closet for a stuffed monkey I had given her when I was five, and she'd knocked over a tall stack of boxes. Pictures had spilled out onto the floor, and Aunt Erma and I had shoved them back into the boxes haphazardly and stacked them back up. When I told her that she could scan them all so they'd be available digitally, she looked at me as if I'd grown a second head.

She seemed content with sorting the photos by date, so we left her upstairs with her very diligent guard dog, Mitzy, while my mother and I worked in the pie shop.

Mr. Barnes didn't greet me with his usual wide smile, but he gave me a hug and squeezed me tightly.

"You're probably busy. I'll just sit here with the paper."

"I'm never too busy for you," I said, carrying two coffees out to the table where he was sitting.

He smiled. I set a steaming mug in front of him. His eyes looked a little watery through his glasses and he sniffed a couple times before taking a sip of coffee.

"What's on your mind today?" I asked.

"This time of year ..." He trailed off. "I love it, and I hate it. My wife loved it."

A tear fell down his cheek, and I swallowed hard trying to keep any from coming to me. I knew he had been married. Flora had told me once. I knew his wife had died ten years ago, but I didn't know much more than that. Mr. Barnes didn't talk about her often. I think it was too painful. I'd never asked him questions because I didn't want to seem nosy and upset him. Today he was in the mood to talk though.

"I still have all the boxes of decorations that she used to put all over our house, but I can't use them." He stared into his coffee. "I've tried taking them out of the storage room before, but every time I do, all the memories come rushing back. Happy memories, you know." He looked at me, blinking a few times.

I nodded.

"But then the sadness hits harder than ever, and I usually shove the boxes back in the room until the next year when I do it all over again."

"The holidays can be tough," I said, thinking of my

dad. I always thought about him this time of year. About what the holidays would be like if he were still here. They had always felt so empty after he died. Probably because that marked our separation with Aunt Erma too. With the four of us, the house had always been bustling and happy, but when it had been just the two of us, me and my mother, it had felt empty and quiet. That was what I remembered most. How quiet it had been. Even when we'd played Christmas music on the radio, it had never been loud enough to cover up the quiet. My mother had tried to make up for it. She really had, but I knew she was sad too. Sometimes she'd invited people to celebrate with us, but it had usually just reminded us that we were celebrating with the wrong people. The last few years had been a little better as Josh had joined us for the holidays when he couldn't get home to his family in Texas. He'd filled some of the quiet.

"I just can't figure out why the universe took her away, but left me behind."

"I'm sure your wife was amazing, but you're amazing too." I reached over and put my hand on top of his. "It doesn't always make sense."

"She would have loved you," he said. "With magic we're even closer to the other side than most people are. Do you feel that more now?"

"Maybe. Sometimes. A little," I said.

"You should come to my yoga class on Thursday nights," he said. "We go deep into meditation. That's when I feel closest to my wife. Maybe you would feel closer to your dad too."

"I'll try that," I said. "I like the idea of being closer to him. I wonder if I could get my mother to come."

"I've worked hard trying to get her to come to my classes. So far, she's refused. Sometimes with fairly colorful language. She is the definition of someone who could use yoga in her life," he said.

"I do not disagree with that statement," I said with a chuckle. I looked at him for a minute. He was staring at a spot on the table. His lip was quivering. "I'm sorry about your wife."

He met my gaze. His eyes were full of tears now. Mine were too.

"I'm sorry about your dad."

I hugged Mr. Barnes, and we both cried for a minute together. When he pulled away, he told me a joke about fish, and I told him a joke about doughnuts. We were laughing and on our second cup of coffee by the time the rest of the Morning Pie Crew arrived.

Later in the day, my mother was in the kitchen rearranging the fridge. She had everything out on the counter and was sorting things by item and expiration date. Aunt Erma sat at the desk in the back of the kitchen and made a paper-clip chain. "I'm going to take Aunt Erma out to run an errand with me," I told her. "Trust me, it's important," I added when my mother started to protest.

"Why would you take her with you?" she pressed.

"Because I need her for this errand," I said. I studied a bag of apples on the counter.

"It seems reckless to take her out in her condition."

"I drank straight out of that milk carton," Aunt Erma chimed in.

"I'll be careful," I promised.

"Are you taking anyone else with you?"

I shook my head just as Aunt Erma nodded. She disappeared upstairs and returned moments later carrying Mitzy.

"See? We're all set. We have a guard dog." I smiled angelically at my mother.

She pursed her lips and let out a "hmph" sound in case by some miracle I had possibly missed her disapproval.

"Okay, Aunt Erma," I said once we were in the car. "Where is the magic tree?"

"I don't like this car," she said.

"I'm going to start driving, and maybe you can give me directions?"

"I've only been in love once before."

I sighed. This had to work. The magic wasn't wearing off, and I needed Aunt Erma back. As much as I wanted to learn about her life since we'd been apart for so long, I didn't want to learn about it this way.

I merged into traffic on the highway. It was busier than usual, probably with holiday travelers going to visit family. I was betting not too many people were searching for a magical tree to break a truth spell. I turned up the music to keep Aunt Erma from divulging too much about her love life again.

"Is that the right exit?" I pointed to a sign at the side of the road.

"One of my favorite words to try and say after a few glasses of wine is 'colloquialism.'"

"Come on, Aunt Erma, this is important!" My hands gripped the steering wheel tightly. I took the exit, hoping the results would be different this time.

Something in the rear-view mirror made me turn the radio off. It was a couple cars back, but there was no doubt it was the same dark green car that I had suspected was following me last time.

"Oh no, what should I do?" I spoke under my breath. If it was the IMPs I didn't want to lead them straight to the magic tree. What if it was just someone who lived off this exit? I didn't want to abandon my mission for something as silly as that.

"We should go home now," Aunt Erma said.

It was the first truly coherent thing she'd said since put under the spell.

"But what about the tree?"

"I've done some things I'm not proud of," she said, looking at Mitzy.

"What does that mean?" I started heading back toward Hocus Hills. I'd lost sight of the green car.

"I don't want you to ever find out." We sat in silence for a minute before Aunt Erma reached over and turned up the radio. "This is my favorite song to dance naked to in my apartment," she offered.

I really had to figure out a way to break the spell.

Mr. Barnes called to ask if I could come take a look at the heater in the yoga studio. I could practically hear him batting his eyelashes through the phone. I grabbed my tool bag and headed over there during a lull in the action at the pie shop. My mother had everything under control, and Aunt Erma seemed happy to be back at her task of sorting photos in the apartment.

When I stepped inside the studio, I wasn't greeted with the usual blast of warm air. Mr. Barnes was sitting in the corner watching television on his small flat-screen TV. He switched it off when I walked in.

"I'm so glad you could come," he said. "Lena tried to fix it, but she couldn't figure out what was wrong. For the last week it's been acting strangely. Sometimes it was running hot, sometimes it was running cold, and finally it just stopped running altogether. I've had to try to convince the classes the last couple days that this is a new kind of yoga. Lukewarm yoga instead of hot yoga. I don't think they're buying it."

"Hopefully I can get you back up and running," I said. The heater was by the ceiling, and Mr. Barnes went to the closet to pull out a step stool for me. I climbed up and unscrewed the corners, so I could lift the front panel off.

I got to work, and he made small talk. I usually liked to work alone, so I could focus, but I didn't want to be rude and ask him to leave his own studio.

"How's your magical education going?" he asked.

"It's been a bit hit and miss." I stepped off the stool to grab some pliers. "I seem to only get half the spells right. Everyone says I'm powerful, but apparently you can't always make up for in power what you lack in knowledge."

"That's very true." Mr. Barnes had pulled a rag out of the closet and was dusting the shelves around the studio now.

"Aunt Erma's a patient teacher though."

"She's a powerful woman too," he said. "Does she ever talk about where her power comes from?"

I hit the test button on the heater and hot air blew into my face. "I think I got you back up and running," I said. I ignored his question and hoped he wouldn't ask it again. Then I stepped down to get away from the hot air. I let it run for a minute, watching it closely for any signs that it might falter. I could feel Mr. Barnes watching me out of the corner of my eye. Once I was satisfied that the heater was fixed, I turned it off, grabbed the cover, and screwed it back in.

"Do you think Aunt Erma expects me to stay in Hocus Hills?" I asked.

He looked a little taken aback. "I don't know if she expects anything from you, but I think she'd like you to stay." I nodded, my brow furrowed as I tightened the last screw.

168

He thanked me for my help as I headed out the door.

"Will I see you for class tonight?" he asked hopefully.

"I think so," I said non-committally.

After the steamy studio, the gust of cold air hit me hard as I stepped outside. I jogged back to the pie shop and burst in through the back door.

My mother was standing inside next to the sink. She held the phone in one hand and her other hand was on her hip. I'd seen that stance before. It was never good. She hung up the phone and glared at me.

"Hey, Mom," I said cheerfully. "How's Aunt Erma doing?"

"I just talked to Nina, and she said you were offered a job at Top-Notch Construction," she said accusingly.

"How did she even know that?" I set down my tool bag at the edge of the desk at the back and poked at the pile of mail.

"Her son-in-law is Buster's daughter's lawyer," she said. "People talk."

Wow, and I thought that was just in small towns. "Yes, he offered me a job," I said.

"Why didn't you tell me?" she asked.

"Because I don't know if I'm going to take it," I said. I picked up a pen from a jar on the desk and twirled it between my fingers.

"What do you mean? Of course, you're going to take it." She began furiously wiping down the counters.

"I want more time here, with all of this." I pointed my pen around the kitchen.

"You can come here and visit."

"You know, some people might consider a thirty-two-year-old to be old enough to make her own decisions."

"Some thirty-two-year-olds would make the *right* decisions." She was now scrubbing an imaginary spot on the counter so hard, I thought she might hurt herself.

I opened my mouth, about to say something completely rational and profound, but Mitzy began barking before I could speak. I ran upstairs, my mother close behind me. We burst through the door.

"Aunt Erma, what's wrong?" I asked breathlessly.

"She has to go outside." She pointed at Mitzy, not even glancing up from her pictures. My mother and I looked at each other for a minute. Our fight would have to be put on hold. I took Mitzy outside.

That evening, I stepped inside the yoga studio for the meditation class. All my shivering muscles relaxed in the warmth. I was happy but not surprised the heater was still working. I looked over at Mr. Barnes, and he gave me a thumbs-up. I began to shed all the layers I had put on over my leggings and tank top. Only four of us had signed up for the class. The two other women worked at the Mexican restaurant. I think the man had come into the pie shop once or twice. I recognized his wavy blond hair and easy smile. The other three looked a lot calmer than I felt. Mr. Barnes had lit candles around the room. There was soothing guitar music playing softly.

"Everyone go ahead and grab your yoga mat and sit down," he said. "Be close to your neighbors. You can feed off each other's energies." I rolled out my yoga mat in the far corner.

I had been to some of Mr. Barnes's yoga classes before, but this time I felt an anxious fluttering in my stomach. When I came to the regular yoga classes, I accepted that I was going to make a fool of myself. I'd try to do the tree pose, then yell "Timber," and fall to the ground. Then I would spend most of the class dreaming about the part at the end when we'd get to lie on the floor.

The stakes were higher this time. This time I wanted to feel closer to my dad.

Mr. Barnes began to walk us through some gentle stretches and breathing exercises. I really wished I hadn't had three cups of coffee before coming here. I could feel my feet twitching even after he had told us to lie down on our backs perfectly still on our mats.

"Just stop all movement." I heard his voice closer to me. I curled my toes, scolding them for their unruly behavior. "Deep breath in and begin to feel all your tension slide out of your body."

I took the breath in and slowly let it out. Hey, it was working. I felt some of the tension and energy in my muscles drift away. "Take another deep breath and focus on slowly inhaling until your lungs are full, and gently release your exhale. Focus only on your breath. The room is warm. You are safe. In here there are no to-do lists. In here there are no expectations. There is just you." His voice was smooth and low.

I tried to be in the moment and not to think about all the pies I had to bake or the apartment I had to find or the presents I had to buy. I really wanted this to work, so I tried *not* to think about how badly I wanted this to work. I felt myself sliding deeper down in my mind. Was I falling asleep? I listened to Mr. Barnes's voice, but I wasn't really paying attention anymore. I was just thinking about my dad.

Dad, where are you? I thought.

Suddenly I saw the highway in front of me. I was zooming along. Was I meditating right? I exited and took a turn down a dirt road. Wait, this was familiar. I was heading towards the magic tree.

"Well, this is unexpected." I heard a voice that was definitely not my father's. My eyes were still closed, but a face popped up in my mind. A woman's face. She looked vaguely familiar, but I couldn't quite put my finger on it.

"Who are you?" I asked.

She scoffed. "Like you don't know." She rolled her eyes and at once I knew who she reminded me of.

"You're Alice's sister," I said.

"That's right. The one and only Nellie." She struck a pose. Her voice had an edge to it. With her dark hair and sharp eyes, she really did look like an evil fairy from a fairy tale.

"I'm not here to see you," I said. I tried to pull myself out. I listened for Mr. Barnes's voice, but I couldn't hear it anymore. "Wake up," I told myself. "Please, wake up. This is just a dream." But nothing. I was still there in front of Nellie. She looked amused.

"Are you done?" she asked.

"I don't want to talk to you," I said.

"Sorry, Cookie, you're on my turf now," she said. "This conversation is over when I say it is."

"What do you want?" I asked.

"You know Erma's secret," she said.

"That she loves pickles?" I asked. I was listening hard for Mr. Barnes's voice. I felt desperate as I tried to stop my thoughts from showing the road. I tried to move away from Nellie, but I was stuck. Nothing was working. I needed to get out of this state.

"I may not have accomplished all the things that I wanted to in the mortal world, but I can still show the IMPs where to find Erma's secret," Nellie said. She was fishing. She didn't even know what the secret was. I tried not to think about the tree.

"Show me!" she cried.

A map appeared in the air for a second. She looked smug, and I yelled and lunged at her.

"Susie! Susie!" Someone was calling my name. They sounded panicked. It wasn't Nellie's voice.

Suddenly I realized I was lying on the ground. I cracked an eye open. Mr. Barnes was standing over me with fear in his eyes. I felt out of breath and confused. I looked around, and the rest of the class was all staring at me.

"What?" I asked innocently.

"You were yelling, and you wouldn't wake up," he said. His voice was still higher pitched than normal, but he looked more relieved now that I was talking to him.

"I must have dozed off," I lied. "I think I was having a bad dream. Sorry, everyone." The rest of the class exchanged raised eyebrows, and I sat up.

"I'm going to call your mother," Mr. Barnes said. He stood up to get the phone.

"That's not necessary. I have to go." I rolled up my mat and grabbed my pile of clothes. I was out the door before he could stop me.

Chapter 12

Dear Elodie,

I have this co-worker who won't stop clearing her throat. She does it loudly all day long! I've resorted to humming to try to block out the disgusting noise. Besides humming the tunes to every musical I've ever heard, how do I get her to stop?

Sincerely,
Battle of the Noise

Dear Battle of the Noise,

I highly recommend you talk to your co-worker! I have a feeling you'll make some headway. If all else fails, invest in some noise-cancelling headphones.

Ask and I'll Answer,

Elodie

I ran straight to my car. I was shivering by the time I slid into the driver's seat because I was still wearing just my tank top and leggings. I threw on my sweatshirt and sweat-pants. I had to get to the tree first.

I started up my car and sped down the road. Heads turned. I knew I shouldn't be drawing this much attention to myself. The roads were still a little slippery after yester-day's snow, so I slowed down a fraction. I wouldn't be able to save Aunt Erma if I got into a car accident.

I had a feeling I would have some explaining to do once I got back. No doubt Mr. Barnes had called my mother. I would have to worry about that later. For now I went back to the things I saw during my meditation. I easily found the right exit this time. I wondered if Nellie was able to tell the IMPs what she knew right away. Aunt Erma had some pretty serious protection spells around the tree, but I wasn't sure it would be enough to keep them away if they went right to it.

I shuddered a little at the thought of Nellie hanging out inside my mind. How could I be sure she wasn't still in there somewhere? I would have to ask Aunt Erma when I got back.

The sun was beginning to lower in the sky as I turned onto the dirt road. I pressed the gas pedal a little harder. I really wanted to get out of the woods before dark. I knew exactly where to pull over. I jumped out of the car and ran in the direction of the tree. It was almost as though it was calling me. It was hard to run through the deep drifts. I had to lift my feet really high as my shoes were filling with snow.

Finally, there it was still decorated and beautiful. I let out a strangled sob of relief. I approached it slowly, as though it might attack me without Aunt Erma. The leaves just rustled in the wind. The snow inside my shoes was beginning to harden into ice.

"What do I need to make her better?" I mused aloud.

A branch near my head shook dangling leaves in my face. I carefully pulled a couple off and put them in my pocket. Then I heard a slight scratching noise and I noticed a corner of the bark had come up. I scraped off a small chunk with my car keys.

"Thank you," I whispered to the tree.

I don't know if I heard it or if I felt it first, but suddenly I knew that I wasn't alone. The hair on the back of my neck stood up. A twig snapped nearby. I couldn't see anyone through the trees, but it was getting darker and hard to make out much of anything. I held my breath and listened. All I could hear was my heart pounding in my chest.

Could it be an animal? I tried to remember what to do if I saw a bear. One kind of bear you were supposed to run from and one you were supposed to play dead for. Which one was which? Were there even bears in these woods? I wished I'd watched more of the nature channel and less reality television.

I was crouched down ready to scream and run because those seemed like the best options, when I heard what sounded like a dinosaur bounding through the woods. Fight or flight, fight or flight, I debated. I decided to hide next to the tree trunk, even though it was far too skinny to cover my body. I hoped that the magic would protect me.

A dark brown creature streaked past me. What was that? A coyote? A lion? A dragon? I was almost delirious with fear. I crouched closer to the tree trunk, and I could feel the magic. It tingled up my arm and through my body, warming me from the inside out. I no longer thought my feet were going to freeze and snap off. I closed my eyes and wished for everything to be okay so I could get back to Aunt Erma.

I could hear crashing through the woods and then a man's voice yelled, "Aaah, run!"

My eyes snapped open. I still couldn't see anyone between the trees. More crashing, and I shivered despite the magic.

The sound was coming towards me now. I pulled out my phone, thinking that I should at least call my mother and tell her where to find my body if I didn't make it back, but I didn't get a signal way out here. Why did I decide to go to the magic tree alone? So what if it was a huge secret?

I tried not to scream as the crashing got closer. I didn't know who was still out in the woods. Then I saw him. A large dark brown dog running towards me. I held very still. Maybe he wouldn't see me. The dog came bounding up and sat at my feet, tail wagging furiously. I cautiously checked him for a collar, but he wasn't wearing one. I looked behind him, but he seemed to be alone.

"Where's your family?" I asked quietly. Clearly, I'd spent too much time with Mitzy and now expected all dogs to understand me.

He leaned his head against my leg, and I scratched him behind his ears.

"Thanks for your help, but shoo. You should go home now," I said. I had to get out of these woods before it was pitch black.

I jogged back towards the car with magical tree bits in my pocket and ice bits crunching in my shoes. Suddenly I was face down in the snow. Ouch. I must have tripped over a tree branch. When I sat up, I was looking into two big brown eyes. The dog was following me.

"Go home," I said again, a little more harshly, as I continued to the car a little slower now. He ignored me and stayed close.

When I got back to the car, I opened the door, and the dog leapt in before I could stop him.

"Hey," I cried, but he didn't seem to mind my protests. He just wagged his tail. "Yeah, you're funny. Now come on." I tried all the dog tricks I had learned from my few weeks with Mitzy. Excited voice. Firm voice. Ignoring him. But nothing worked. The dog remained firmly planted in the car. I tried to push him out, but it seemed as if he weighed a thousand pounds. From the look on his face, he wasn't at all bothered by my frustration.

"Fine, I'll take you home later." I gave in. I had to get this stuff back to Aunt Erma. The dog wagged his tail.

Once I was in the driver's seat, he licked my cheek. "Not cool, dog," I said, wiping my face off with the sleeve of my jacket.

By the time we got back to Hocus Hills, the dog was curled up sleeping in the back seat. I decided to worry about the new creature later.

"What in the world?" my mother asked when she saw the unfamiliar dog. He'd followed me inside as if he belonged there.

"Don't ask," I said flatly.

"Stop right there," my mother said. The dog sat down.

I turned toward her and tilted my head. "What?" I asked brightly.

"Mr. Barnes called." Of course he had. Tattletale. "Would you care to explain to me what happened at the yoga studio?"

"I'll admit, it got pretty wild. There was stretching and music and even—" I paused dramatically "—candles burning." My mother was not amused. I let out a frustrated sigh. "Nothing happened. I was tired. I fell asleep. Then I had to run some errands. I'm going to go take a quick nap now. I'll be back soon to help close up." The dog got up to happily follow me upstairs.

"We're not done talking about this," my mother called. "And where on earth did that dog come from?"

Mitzy ran to greet me when I walked through the door, but stopped dead in her tracks when she saw I wasn't alone. She sized him up. He was easily twice her size. She ran around him, sniffed him and jumped on him. He lay down, his tail wagging, and watched her run around in excited circles.

Aunt Erma was still sitting at the table going through photos. She looked up when I approached her. "Tea," she announced with a firm nod.

"Is that what I do with this?" I asked, pulling the slightly squished leaves and chunk of bark out of my pocket.

"I like tea," she said.

"I'm going to make some," I said. I hoped that she would direct me at some point if I was doing it wrong, so I explained every step of the way. "I'm boiling some water," I said. "Then I'm going to steep these leaves and this bark in the water."

She tilted her head at me. "When I was nine, I used to write love letters to the actor from that monkey movie."

"Okay," I said. "After it's steeped for a few minutes, I'm going to strain it and pour it into a mug."

She winked at me. "Right on, sugar," she said.

The dogs had pulled all the blankets and pillows off the sofa, and they were now gleefully rolling on them. I yelled at them to stop, but those same ears that could hear a treat bag open from a mile away suddenly couldn't hear me.

"Would you like honey, or does that mess with the tree's magic?" I asked Aunt Erma.

"I like to lick the edge of the honey jar when it drips," she said. I really hoped this tea worked. I couldn't handle all these truths for too much longer. I made a mental note not to use the honey anymore.

I let the leaves and the bark steep while I made up a spell to break the spell on Aunt Erma. She had told me that intention was very important when casting a spell, so I made sure my intention was pure and hoped that would be enough. Plus, the tree seemed to love Aunt Erma, so maybe it would work with me to free her from this evil spell. I paused for a second. It had been just a few weeks since I'd learned about magic and how it was real – a fact I hadn't even considered since I was a child, but here we were. I was believing that a tree could have good or bad intentions. I shook my head a little. Life was funny sometimes.

Once I thought the tea had brewed long enough, I carefully poured it into a green and blue caterpillar mug and handed it to her.

"Please drink this," I said. She looked at it and then looked at me. I was afraid for a moment she wouldn't drink it and breathed a sigh of relief as she took a small sip. She wrinkled her nose and set the mug down on the counter. Apparently magic-tree tea didn't taste good. I added some honey, trying not to touch the sides of the jar. I handed the mug back to her. She took another sip and smiled. She finished the magic tea.

I held my breath and watched her carefully. I was hoping to see sparkles around her or hear some magic music or something, but nothing.

"Thank you." Aunt Erma sighed. "It's good to be back."

I threw myself at her and she dropped the teacup. It shattered on the floor.

"Oops," I said. Mitzy made a running leap and was in Aunt Erma's arms as soon as I was out of them. "It worked! It worked!" I danced around. Our new dog friend joined me as I danced a victory lap around the living room.

My mother rushed in brandishing a rolling pin. "What's happening? What's wrong?"

"Aunt Erma's back," I said, presenting her with a flourish of my arm.

Aunt Erma smiled at my mother. "That was truly an awful spell," she said. My mother ran towards her.

"Careful," I warned as my mother got close to the sharp bits of ceramic. "Mitzy broke a teacup." I pointed to the ground, and Mitzy gave me a death stare.

I felt a huge wave of relief now that we had Aunt Erma back to her usual self. Now we just had to stop the IMPs, and we could really focus on Christmas.

Chapter 13

Dear Elodie,

I made a mistake. Six years ago I told the guy I'd just started seeing that I loved seahorses. I don't know why I said it, it just came out. I didn't think much of it until he bought me a seahorse necklace for my birthday. That was very sweet. For the next holiday he bought me a six-foot-tall seahorse statue. We're still together, and things have escalated. One of my friends told me that he plans to come into my house while I'm at work and put up seahorse wallpaper. That's too much, right? I shudder when I think about their beady eyes staring at me all the time. How do I stop the madness?

Sincerely,

Seahorse Nightmare

Dear Seahorse Nightmare,

Things have ESCALATED from a SIX-FOOT seahorse statue? Oh dear! You need to talk to him right

185

away. If you're worried about hurting his feelings, just say you've recently decided that you love giraffes more (or some other animal that you actually love). You should also take an inventory of the relationship and see how often he is surprising you with things that actually horrify you. A little white lie here and there is one thing, but a relationship that doesn't have open communication could lead to bigger problems down the road.

Ask and I'll Answer,

Elodie

Word spread fast, and the Morning Pie Crew was in the front of the shop laughing and hugging Aunt Erma in no time.

Lena pulled out a bottle of champagne and six champagne flutes from her giant yellow purse.

"To family, friends, and broken curses," Aunt Erma said, clinking glasses with everyone. I served everyone slices of chocolate coconut cream pie.

"What's the name of your new friend?" Flora asked.

I was confused until she explained. "That dog you brought home. What's his name?" she asked.

"I don't know," I said. "I'm waiting for his family to claim him. They'll know what his name is."

"Dear," Aunt Erma chimed in. "He's yours. You're his. It's a special magic that brings together a person and an animal, and you two belong together. You should figure out what his name is." The dog wagged his tail at me.

"Sure," I told her, though part of me was still hoping someone would show up to take him home.

"And you can't just assign him a name," Mr. Barnes said.

"You have to say different names and sounds until he reacts. That's how you figure out what he's supposed to be called," Lena explained. I looked around at all of them, expecting one of them to crack and tell me they were just kidding, but they all looked back at me with earnest gazes. Even my own mother.

"Right," I said slowly.

The minute everyone was distracted by how cute Mitzy and No Name were together, I pulled Aunt Erma into the kitchen and told her about Nellie appearing while I meditated and the person in the woods near the magic tree.

Her brow was wrinkled. "I should go put some extra protection spells on the tree just in case," she said.

"I'll go with you," I said.

"No, you need to stay here and keep everyone distracted so they don't notice that I'm gone." She grabbed her keys and was out the back door before I could protest.

"Where's Erma?" were, of course, the first words out of Lena's mouth the second I came back from the kitchen.

"She just had to ..." I wracked my brain for an excuse "... run upstairs to the bathroom," I finished lamely. "Her last meal was not sitting so well." I patted my stomach and gave a sympathetic grimace.

They accepted my explanation without further questions.

Sorry, Aunt Erma, I thought.

Aunt Erma returned quickly. She was a little flushed as she rushed back into the room.

"How are you feeling?" Mr. Barnes asked.

"Fine," she said.

I raised my eyebrows and gave her a look that I hoped would say, "Are you sure about that?" I patted my stomach a little.

"Did you drink that ginger tea I brought you?" I asked.

"Oh yes, that was extremely helpful," she said smoothly. "I'm all better now." She took a sip of her champagne.

She's a skilled liar, I thought.

Henry came in. "I heard there's a celebration going on," he said.

Lena poured him some champagne, and the topic switched from Erma's newly broken spell to Flora's birthday dinner the next night. Her birthday had been shoved to the back burner with everything else that was happening, but now that Aunt Erma was back, they'd decided the show must go on.

"We can use that time to strategize a little more," Flora said. "We have to stop the IMPs so we can stop living in fear."

"Susie's friend Josh is going to be there," my mom reminded everyone.

I noticed Henry's eyebrows go up ever so slightly, but the rest of his face remained neutral.

"We'll have to be discreet, then," Flora said.

The next day was busy with preparations for Flora's birthday dinner and making pies for the shop. Customers buzzed with the excitement of the upcoming holidays. They were able to focus more on Christmas and less on the potential evil takeover of our town.

I was in charge of taking Flora Christmas shopping. Apparently if she was allowed to remain too close to the vicinity of the party, she was at risk of helping with preparations. That was against the rules.

A gentle snow was falling when I crossed the street to meet her at the bookshop. I turned my face up to the flakes and felt a small ripple of excitement. Flora's birthday party was offering a preview of Christmas. Even the pre-preparations that were happening before I left were already loud and enthusiastic. I had always thought Christmas was magical, but this year was the first time I'd be celebrating with more than a few people and I couldn't wait.

"I'll be right there, Susie," she called from somewhere in the store. I was never quite sure how she knew it was me.

I browsed for a few minutes before Flora appeared all bundled up and ready to go out.

"Are you sure they don't need any help?" she asked, peering across the street.

"They're just fine." I grabbed her arm and steered her in the opposite direction. "Where would you like to go?"

"Sally's Gifts-n-Things," she said.

Sally's was a multi-story shop on the other side of town. She had bins and shelves full of all the random crap that no one ever needed, but you suddenly felt you wanted more than anything in the world the minute you walked through the door.

"Who do you have left to shop for?" I asked.

"Oh, I've had everyone done for weeks now," she said.

"Are all of your gifts wrapped already too?"

"Of course," she said, as though she couldn't imagine a universe in which someone would still be Christmas shopping this close to Christmas.

"I still have to find something for Henry." I looked up to the sky, suddenly feeling a wave of guilt.

"Well, we'll find him something today." She patted my arm reassuringly.

Walking into Sally's was like an assault on the senses after being in the peaceful snow outside. The front of the store was packed with items that demanded attention with their flashing lights, Christmas songs, and dance moves.

I glanced over at Flora, who to my surprise looked delighted. She immediately went over to a table and pushed every button to make every item on the table dance or talk or spin around. I wandered back to a quieter section of the store. I picked up a small wind-up car and quickly set it down again when I realized I was thinking what a perfect present that would be for Josh. It looked just like one he'd had when he was a kid, complete with a red and blue stripe down the side. He showed me a picture once. He had lost the car, but still talked about it and how many fond memories he had of playing with it in his driveway.

I was here for Henry. Think of Henry. I glanced back at the car as though it were at fault for my momentary lapse in judgement.

I wandered around the store with a growing sense of panic. Nothing in here seemed right for Henry. What in the world was I supposed to get him? If I knew what he'd gotten me, I could better gauge what to get him. Maybe he'd just bought me a mug. That would take some of the pressure off. But from what I'd heard around town, Henry was a world class gift-giver.

I was sorting through a bin of doll clothes because I'd gone completely off my rocker and was hoping something in there would inspire me when I heard Sally boom, "What can I help you with?" Sally was just as over the top as her store. She was a large woman with wild red hair, dark eyes, and a voice that would fill any room. Her outfits usually consisted of so many patterns and colors that it was hard for the eye to take in.

"Just looking for a gift for Henry," I said. She looked down at the bin of doll clothes and then back up at me with her eyebrows raised. I dropped the pair of tiny lace bloomers I was holding and took a step back.

"You might have better luck over in that section." She pointed to a cluster of shelves on the other side of the store.

"I like your necklace." I paused to examine the green teardrop necklace she was wearing.

"This old thing?" She waved me off and tucked the necklace into her shirt. "It's nothing."

I felt as if I'd hit a nerve. Maybe it was from an old lover. I shrugged it off and went over to the shelves. I had to focus on finding the perfect gift.

An hour later Flora and I emerged from the shop. She had an armload of bags.

"I thought you had all your Christmas shopping done," I said.

"I do," she responded. "These are birthday presents for the year."

How in the world could she have Christmas and birthdays taken care of while I was on the edge of a nervous breakdown just from buying one present tonight? I glanced into my own bag, pathetically small compared to Flora's haul.

"I'm not sure about this," I said. I reached in and touched it. Sure, it was soft, but a sweater? How clichéd could I get? I tried to picture Henry's face when he opened it. I was sure he would be appreciative, which would make the lameness of the present all the more painful.

"It's a good gift," Flora assured me. Her assurance felt a little stiff, as though she was trying too hard.

I have to admit, I would have been more excited for dinner if I weren't so nervous about Josh and Henry sitting in the same room. I could already feel the tension, and neither of them had arrived yet. Maybe it will be fine, I told myself. Right, and maybe Santa and his elves will come to dinner.

I had been dying to ask if Santa was real, but I was pretty sure I would never live down the ridiculing if he wasn't. Maybe I could try asking Flora some time. She was least likely to laugh in my face.

My new dog friend was eager to help. I was in charge of the salad. The kitchen in the apartment was small, and as I walked from one side to the other he tried to anticipate my every step so he could take it first. I didn't know if he was trying to help or trying to kill me.

Flora's only request for the night was that everyone dress festively. Once the salad was made, I changed into a red tunic and green leggings and patted myself on the back for my Christmassy outfit.

My mother, of course, was in a classy maroon skirt and white blouse. Aunt Erma wore a sparkly red jumpsuit with a large Santa pin, or, as I mentally called it, "My Segue into the Santa Conversation" pin. She had gold bells hanging from every button on her jumpsuit, and she topped the outfit off with her large antlers.

Everyone had done an amazing job decorating the front of the pie shop while I was off distracting Flora. They'd blown up balloons, hung streamers, and draped garlands of paper flowers around the pie display case. Lena had brought over a banner that she'd made that said, "Happy Birthday, Flora!", and Mr. Barnes had brought extra fairy lights to wrap around everywhere. The place looked even more magical than usual.

My mother, Aunt Erma, and I were putting the finishing touches on the room while we waited for everyone to arrive. Much to their delight, the dogs had been invited to join the fun tonight. Mitzy ran around sniffing every corner of the pie shop in search of stray crumbs, and No Name set up camp in front of the food table. He lay there with his head between his paws looking pitifully at anyone who made eye contact with him, as though he hadn't just eaten a giant bowl of dog food upstairs.

"While we wait for everyone, let's get this party started," Aunt Erma said, hitting play on the boombox. I had tried to get Aunt Erma to upgrade her music system a couple weeks ago, but I hadn't got very far.

"You could go digital and make playlists of your favorite songs," I had mentioned to her.

"But I have my favorite songs on CDs," she'd replied.

"With digital music, you don't have to keep switching your CDs to hear all your favorite songs in a row."

"Why are you trying to take away my CDs?"

"This would be even better than CDs."

Blank stare. "Never mind."

"Holly Jolly Christmas" began playing and Aunt Erma and I danced between the tables. Mitzy jumped around our feet, her tail wagging excitedly. The other dog just watched us from his spot sprawled on the ground. My mother suddenly got very busy rearranging crackers on a tray, but I caught her doing a little shimmy when the tempo really picked up.

Flora and Lena arrived together. Lena's sweater had a Christmas tree across the front complete with lights that lit up. Flora was dressed up head to toe as an elf. "I'm wearing the clothes of my ancestors," she said.

"Flora, your ancestors didn't dress up in green pointy hats and bell shoes," Aunt Erma said.

"Don't ruin my fun," she replied. She did a little jig and the bells on her shoes jingled.

Violet came in a dark green business suit. I had a feeling that was the most festive thing she owned. Mr. Barnes arrived with his bright red fedora and a matching vest over a bright green shirt and brown pants. He topped off the look with a snowman bow tie.

Josh was close behind him. "I didn't have anything festive enough," he said. "So, Mr. Barnes lent me these." He took off his jacket, revealing glittery candy-cane suspenders.

"Classy," Flora said approvingly.

I greeted Josh cautiously. I was pretty sure he would be well behaved tonight, but the last thing I was ready to handle was a public proclamation of love. Lena and Flora seemed almost giddy and were watching Josh closely. I think they were enjoying the show.

Henry texted that he was going to be late. Some fiasco was happening at the nursing home. "Don't ask," he texted. It must be bad.

We poured drinks for everyone and sat down. I carefully seated myself between my mother and Lena. My mother hopped up so quickly, I was surprised she didn't get whiplash.

"Josh, sit here. I'm going to take a spot closer to the kitchen, so I can keep an eye on the food," she said smoothly.

I wanted to glare at her, but it seemed too obvious. Josh sat down next to me. I pretended to be engrossed in a conversation Mr. Barnes and Flora were having about his ingrown toenail.

"Merry Flora's Birthday," Josh said, bumping his knee gently against mine.

"Yeah, you too," I said. I smiled tentatively at him. Maybe he wanted to talk to me because he wanted to tell me that he'd been wrong when he'd professed his love to me. It was as if some huge mistake had been made, and he just wanted to be friends again.

"Remember last year when the Butler family hired us to hang Christmas lights all over their house, including around the toilet in the bathroom?" he asked.

"That part wasn't so bad. I thought the inside of the

closets was a bit excessive though," I said, laughing. Soon we were talking like the old friends we were.

I almost didn't notice when Henry walked in. He was wearing a bright blue sweater with a giant snowflake on it.

"Henry," voices chorused, bringing Josh and I out of our conversation. He looked tired but gave the room a giant smile. He came over and squeezed my shoulder. "Hey, you," he said. Then turned to Josh. "Good to see you again. How are you enjoying our town?"

"I love it here," he said. "The people here are so nice. I really feel welcome."

"That's so great," Henry said, but there was something in his voice that made me think he might not be thrilled Josh was feeling so at home in Hocus Hills.

I glanced up and noticed that Flora, Lena, Violet, Mr. Barnes, and Aunt Erma were all openly watching the conversation. The only thing they were missing was popcorn. At least my mom wasn't gawking, I thought, until I looked over and saw her watching from the kitchen doorway. She was holding a potato masher and an empty bowl.

"Do you need any help in there, Mom?" I asked, jumping out of my chair.

"Let me help too," Henry said. I noticed he shot a look back towards Josh as he followed me.

"Go ahead and take a seat, Mom," I said. I took the masher out of her hand. She hesitated but then went to sit down with Josh. I breathed a sigh of relief, and Henry snuck a quick kiss.

"Be careful," I warned. "That's violating the health code."

"I'll risk the fine," he said, kissing me again.

"How was your day?" I asked.

"It was Christmas cookie baking day," he said with low dread in his voice. "I had to go home and shower before coming here. I had flour in places I didn't know I could have flour."

"Oh no," I laughed.

"It wasn't as bad as your most recent cookie experiences though, so I really can't complain." He helped me drain the potatoes, so we could start mashing them.

"What cookie experiences?" Josh appeared in the doorway of the kitchen.

"I had a minor feud with a woman who owned a cookie shop in town," I said. "She's not here anymore though." I kept my eyes on the mashed potatoes, only glancing up once to see how he was taking my vague story. He just nodded.

"Could you put these on the table?" I asked, holding out the giant bowl.

We all sat down at the crowded table. I sat next to Henry, but directly across from Josh. Flora was at the head of the table.

Flora clinked her wine glass with her knife to get everyone's attention. The group quieted down, except for Lena, who began composing her symphony by clinking all the glasses around her with her knife. She bobbed her head to the beat.

"It's going to be your job to take away her wine glass," Flora told Josh with a wink.

"Oh no, I would never touch another person's wine glass," he said, holding his hands up.

Lena wrapped up her song and gave us all a serene smile. We turned our attention to Flora.

Flora gave a heartfelt toast about how lucky she was to be surrounded by such wonderful friends and family. I glanced around the table. Through my tears I could see I wasn't the only one getting misty-eyed. Henry was using his napkin to wipe away a tear on his cheek, and Mr. Barnes had removed his glasses. Aunt Erma and Lena were both sniffing. Violet was blinking hard. My mother was staring intensely at a spot on the ceiling. Even Josh's brow was wrinkled with emotion. When she was done, we all cheered with tears in our eyes.

Dinner was delicious. The chatter was so loud I could hardly hear the Christmas music in the background.

After everyone helped clear the table, the strategy sessions began. The groups began to rotate so that at least one person was always watching Josh. My mother seemed more than happy to keep him in a magic-free zone. She kept trying to pull me into their conversations. I thought she was still hoping that I would leave this magic life and return home to marry Josh. I wouldn't be surprised if she began calling him "son" after one more glass of red wine.

"The ice show is tomorrow," Violet told me, Henry, Flora, and Aunt Erma while Mr. Barnes regaled Josh and my mother with tales of his last yoga retreat. "They might try something there. It's a big town event. After the snowman-building competition, the last thing we need is to have a bunch of ice skaters attacking the crowd." Lena shuddered at the thought.

We kept rotating into different groups as we made a plan – it was like a giant game of telephone, and the more wine that was consumed, the more jumbled the plan got. In the end I thought Henry and I had volunteered to stake out the ice show and keep an eye out for any IMP activity. Violet recruited Lena and Aunt Erma to help her watch the security-camera feeds from around town, and Flora and Mr. Barnes would drive around town looking for anything strange that the security cameras might miss. I hoped one of us would remember the plan.

"Goodnight, everyone," I said a little too loudly as they all shuffled out the door some time after midnight.

Josh lingered for a minute, but so did Henry. After an awkward moment, Josh said a quick goodbye and left.

"I can't wait to go to the ice show with you," Henry said once we were alone. Well, kind of alone. Aunt Erma was in the kitchen and there were two dogs sitting in the middle of the room, tails thumping as they wagged. Their unblinking eyes stayed fixed on us.

"This would be so much more romantic if we weren't on the lookout for psycho villains," I said.

"We can make it romantic." He gently brushed the hair out of my eyes and put his hand behind my neck, pulling me in for a kiss.

I heard what sounded like a sneeze. Or was it laughter? I really had to get my own place, so my new love life wasn't critiqued from the next room. Henry headed for the door and I turned to clear the table.

"Weren't there still cookies on this plate?" I asked. I held up the now perfectly clean green shiny plate.

"You're right, I thought there were still some," Henry said.

I looked around the room and my eyes landed on the dog, who was gently wagging his tail.

"Did you eat these?" I asked. His tail wagged harder. I looked closer and noticed a dusting of crumbs lining his mouth.

I lifted his lips and checked his teeth. There was definitely a red sprinkle wedged between them.

I didn't know much about dogs, but I was pretty sure they weren't supposed to chow down on ten sugar cookies.

"Aunt Erma," I cried.

Henry knelt down next to me and stroked the dog's head. Aunt Erma ran into the room.

"What do I do? What am I supposed to do? He ate all the cookies!" The dog tilted his head and looked at me with questioning eyes as though not sure what I was worried about.

"He'll probably be okay, but we could take him to the vet," Henry offered.

"I think he'll be fine, but you can bring him to Dr. Silva just to be sure," Aunt Erma said.

"I'll go with her," Henry said. My heart was in my throat. This dog was in my care for less than forty-eight hours and I had already messed up. This didn't set a good precedent. The dog looked completely fine, but I kept having images of him collapsing. I needed a doctor's reassurance.

"Let's go." I ran and grabbed one of Mitzy's leashes. Mitzy sprang up when she saw it. "Sorry, not tonight, Mitz." She humphed and flopped back down, her dagger eyes boring into the other dog. Clearly their relationship was off to a stellar start.

Dr. Silva lived just around the corner from the pie shop, so we decided it would be fastest to walk. Henry called the doctor on our way to let him know we were coming. The dog seemed to be walking fine, but every now and then I could have sworn he twitched in a way that indicated discomfort or impending doom. Dr. Silva was a very patient man with thinning hair and a gentle demeanor. He answered the door in his pajamas. He examined the dog thoroughly, carefully looking in his mouth and ears. He asked some questions, many of which I didn't know the answers to, including the very simple question, "What's his name?" I was feeling useless and panicked.

"He's going to be fine," he assured me.

"Can you just double-check?"

"I have double-checked."

"Can you triple-check?"

"Would you like to leave him here overnight?"

"No." I put my arm around the dog protectively.

"Okay, just keep an eye on him and call me if you have any concerns." Dr. Silva pulled a business card from a nearby desk. I sensed a moment of hesitation before he handed it to me. I realized I'd become the crazy dog lady. I looked down at the dog, who looked back up at me with his big eyes, as though he still couldn't figure out what all the fuss was about.

Henry, the dog, and I walked slowly back to the pie shop. I was worried about forcing the dog to walk too fast in case it upset his stomach.

"Do you think he looks a little woozy?" I asked, craning my neck to examine the dog's face again.

"I think he looks just fine," Henry said. He wrapped his arm around me tightly and I leaned into his warmth. The snow had stopped and most of the clouds had cleared. The stars were twinkling brightly in the sky.

"I wonder if he has a family out there somewhere," I said. The dog looked back at me and wagged his tail.

"I think you're his family now," Henry said. "Would you like me to stay over and help you keep an eye on him?"

"What about Willy?"

"I could bring him."

I had to laugh at that. Three people and three dogs,

especially one as large as Willy, would have Aunt Erma's apartment bursting at the seams.

"Or you could bring him to my house," Henry offered. I had to admit the idea was tempting, but I didn't want to uproot the dog in his delicate state.

"I should probably stay in tonight." I couldn't keep the hint of wistfulness from creeping into my voice.

"Call me if you need anything," Henry said. We were in the alley at the back door of the pie shop now.

"I will," I promised and leaned in to kiss him. His nose was cold against my cheek, but his lips were warm. I heard a strange noise and felt something warm sliding down my leg. I pulled back and looked down to see the dog had thrown up cookies all over my leg. The dog's tail wagged hard and his ears perked up as though he was very proud of his accomplishment. I swallowed, trying not to gag.

"I better go in and clean up," I choked out. Henry looked amused, but was smart enough not to laugh in my presence.

I ran upstairs, the dog close at my heels.

"I'm going to shower," I called to Aunt Erma as I flew past her and into the bathroom.

Once I was clean and in my pajamas, I recounted the night's experience to Aunt Erma. She did not have the same manners as Henry and burst out laughing when I got to the part about the dog throwing up on my leg.

It was getting late so Aunt Erma disappeared into her room to read. Instead of joining her as she usually would, Mitzy stayed in the living room, gazing adoringly at her new friend. Apparently Mitzy had forgiven him for his earlier indiscretions of eating cookies without sharing and stealing her leash. The dark brown dog stared at me as I lay down on the sofa. I reached over and stroked his head, studying his face for any remaining ill effects.

"What's your name, buddy?" I asked. I decided to try Lena's method and began to list names to see if the dog would react. Maybe if I could at least figure the sound out, I could guess his name.

I began to sing the alphabet song. The dog lay down, but kept staring at me. His tail began to wag when I got to G but then I heard a rumbling noise and realized he was just passing gas. Mitzy stood and took a few steps back, but her loving gaze didn't falter.

"Fluffy?" I tried. He closed an eye. "Rover?" He closed the other. I went through Larry, Bob, Gigi, Puppy, Bubba – all without a reaction. I kept going, I began just naming objects in the room. "Phone, Table, Sofa, Rug." All turned out not to be his name. I moved on to food. "Pizza, Pie, Raisin, Margarita, Lemon, Apple, Burrito." No reaction. "Coffee. Cake. Doughnut." At the last one, he opened his eyes. "Doughnut," I tried again. He didn't move, but he watched me.

"It's probably something that starts with a D," Aunt Erma called from the other room.

"Dooey, Darryl, Diego, Declan, Dakota, Daniel," I tried. Mitzy had settled into a spot on the back of the sofa and was now snoring loudly.

While I kept listing D names, I pulled one of Mitzy's tennis balls out from under the sofa. "Do you want to play, Dexter?" I asked. I gently bounced the ball towards him. It hit him in the side, but he didn't even move. Mitzy heard her second favorite toy being used and flew across the room to retrieve it.

"You have to read your doggie handbook, because that's what you're supposed to do." I pointed at Mitzy. He seemed unconcerned.

I looked up D names on the internet and read through the list. By the time I was nearing the end, both dogs were sound asleep. When I said, "Duncan," that all changed. The big dog was on his feet and hurtled towards me, his tail wagging furiously. He got three licks on my face before I was able to sit up and push him away.

Aunt Erma came out of her room looking a little sleepy. "You figured it out?" she asked.

"Yes, I'd like to introduce you to Duncan," I said. Duncan sat at her feet and proudly wagged his tail.

"Hello, Duncan. Nice to officially meet you." She shook his paw in her hand. "That's strange," Aunt Erma said, looking over at the phone table. She hadn't yet fully transitioned to cell phones. She still had a rotary dial phone on a table next to an answering machine. The light was blinking on the machine. "I thought I checked this when I first came upstairs. I didn't hear it ring, did you?" I shook my head. She hit the play button.

I heard an unfamiliar voice say, "Erma, when are you

coming back? We miss you."Aunt Erma went pale and hit the stop button so quickly she almost knocked the machine off the table.

"Who was that?" I asked.

"No one," she said, so quickly I'm surprised she even heard my question. Aunt Erma said goodnight and disappeared into her bedroom.

That was strange.

Chapter 14

Dear Elodie,

The other day I used my boyfriend's phone to make a call because mine was dead. While I was on it, a text came in from a woman he works with. Curiosity got the best of me, and I clicked on the message. I saw that they'd been texting each other for months at all hours, day and night. There's nothing particularly juicy in the messages, just a lot of friendly (and what could be interpreted as flirtatious) banter. This makes me very uncomfortable, but I don't know what to do now.

Do I confront my boyfriend? If I do, I have to admit that I was snooping through his phone. If I don't confront him, I think it will eat away at our relationship. Please help me figure out how to fix this.

Sincerely,
Sorry I Snooped

Dear Sorry I Snooped,
You have to talk to your boyfriend about it. Don't

*make it a confrontation, make it a conversation. You'll
have to admit that you snooped, and you can apologize
for violating his privacy. But tell him that now that it's
out there, you need to talk about it. Most likely, he'll
deny that anything inappropriate is going on, and it's
up to you to decide if you believe him or not. It's possible
for people to have emotional affairs without having a
physical one. You two have to talk about whether or
not you're getting what you want out of your relationship with each other. Problems in a relationship can be
fixed as long as both parties in the relationship are
open to fixing them.*

   Ask and I'll Answer,

Elodie

I stayed up all night watching Duncan sleep. Every time
he twitched or snorted I sat up to examine him closer.
I called Dr. Silva three times to see if certain movements
or stomach gurgles might indicate something more serious
was wrong with Duncan. By the third time, he asked me
to lose his card.

Aunt Erma emerged from her room fully dressed before
the sun was up.

"Who was that voicemail from last night?" I asked.

She waved a dismissive hand. "No one. It's not important." She was out of the door of the apartment before I
could ask any more questions.

I took the dogs outside and fed them breakfast. A small

breakfast for Duncan per Dr. Silva's instructions, much to Duncan's dismay. The dogs snuggled in on the couch while I got ready.

"Keep an eye on him, Mitzy," I said. "I'll be back soon to check on you two."

We had a lot of special holiday orders people were picking up today. Three different people had ordered rum raisin pies. Why anyone would special order that was beyond me. Raisins made me want to gag, so I quickly offered to make the peanut butter silk. My mother made the rum raisin, and Aunt Erma worked on the berry pies. There were a couple of special orders for boysenberry pie and twenty-seven orders for her famous blueberry pie.

The second we unlocked the door, we had customers. The usual midmorning lull never came. People came in to pick up their orders, eat a slice of pie with out-of-town family and friends, and apologetically place last-minute special orders.

I didn't have any time to worry about the strange voice-mail from last night. I was serving customers out front while my mom and Aunt Erma kept baking and washing dishes in the back.

Lena called to ask if we should meet at the pie shop or the hardware store.

I was silent on the other end of the phone.

"You forgot about our appointment, didn't you?" she asked.

"No," I said slowly while wracking my brain.

"I'm taking you apartment hunting," she said.

"Right!" Our conversation from a few days ago came back to me. "I'm not sure if it's a good time though." I told her about everything that was going on.

"There's never a perfect time. Only now," she said. "I'll have you back in no time."

I went into the kitchen. "Can you guys spare me for an hour?"

My mother said, "No," just as Aunt Erma said, "Yes."

"Great, I'll hurry back," I said. I ran upstairs to grab my coat and check on the dogs before rushing out the back door before the conversation could go any further.

I was still feeling a little conflicted about staying in Hocus Hills. Sometimes I missed the bustle of the city, and then there was the wonderful job offer to consider. Then there was Josh. I hadn't decided if he was in the pro column or the con column on the list of reasons to move back to the city.

I decided that it couldn't hurt to see what my apartment options were. I had been sleeping on Aunt Erma's sofa for too long, and, now that I apparently had a dog, the apartment was getting a little crowded. Plus, I'd had one too many dates that included Aunt Erma and Mitzy. Henry had his own house, but his large dog, Willy, wasn't sure that he liked me as much as Henry did. He would sit in the middle of the living room and watch me through narrowed eyes. That was a little unsettling when you were trying to make out on the sofa.

And, of course, it was impossible to have any privacy at a restaurant in a town like Hocus Hills. Henry was well liked, and it was not uncommon for people to stop by our table to chat for five to fifty minutes. I liked the small-town charm, and the fact that people adored Henry, but it was awfully difficult to get into the romantic mood when Bill Carter stopped by to tell us a graphic twenty-minute story about his latest bout of food poisoning. I ended up telling the waitress, "Thanks, but I'm not hungry anymore," when she brought out my bowl of vegetarian chili.

There were a few customers in the store when I got there. Lena was helping a woman pick out a light switch and she came over to me when she was done.

"It looks like you're keeping busy," I said.

"All those little projects that pile up over the course of the year are suddenly getting done because the in-laws are coming to stay for a week, and they expect to have a working doorknob on the bathroom," she said.

"I don't want to take you away from your store," I said.

"Don't worry. Denny's got it covered," she said. Denny was the nineteen-year-old that Lena had hired for the holidays. He was quiet and a little sullen, but his lanky appearance and awkward manner reminded me a little too much of Stan. Because of the resemblance, I usually avoided the hardware store if I knew Denny was working. That was really a tragedy because I loved going to the hardware store.

The second we stepped outside, Lena went into full

real-estate-agent mode. "Don't you just love this time of year?" she asked. "There are no bad views in this town when it's all decorated for the holidays. And everywhere that I'm going to show you is conveniently located near the pie shop and near all the necessities, like the grocery store and the restaurants."

"Lena," I said, laughing. "If you're showing me any apartment in town, I'll be conveniently located near all the necessities."

"Well ..." she sniffed indignantly "... I think you'll like the ones I picked out anyway."

"I'm sure I will," I said. "You don't have to sell me on Hocus Hills."

"I've heard rumors you're still running a little hot and cold on our town," she said. "There's a lot of pressure for me to perform. You should have heard the lecture Flora and Mr. Barnes gave me on the importance of finding you a place that you would love. Even Henry called and told me to pull out all the stops. When I was in the grocery store, Holly wouldn't check me out unless I promised to show you the place over on Sparkle Street." She said all this hardly taking a breath. "Apparently Sparkle Street is an acceptable distance from Holly so that you guys can hang out and still walk home from each other's places after a few glasses of wine without getting lost."

"I see," I said. No wonder Lena was laying it on thick. There was an awful lot of pressure associated with where I lived.

"Erma will probably stop speaking to me once she hears I've taken you out apartment hunting. She doesn't think you should move until after we stop the IMPs." She threw up her arms. "I just can't win sometimes."

"I'm sorry everyone's been giving you such a hard time," I said. I put my arms around her and gave her a big hug.

"It's all right. I can take it," she said with a dramatic toss of her head. "Let's not worry about any of them now, though." She switched back to her realtor voice. "Let's focus on you and what you want."

Lena was right. The first apartment did have wonderful views. It was on the second floor and looked down on the town square. The apartment itself had dingy gray walls and was about the size of a broom closet, but it did have a nice view. Lena kept pointing to the dusty window.

"It's nice," I said, trying to force a smile. We were a little too close to Alice's old cookie shop for my taste. Even though she was gone, her bad vibes still haunted me. I was hoping with enough yoga I could get past my dislike of this corner of the town square. But it wasn't going to happen overnight, so we left that first apartment pretty quickly.

"I thought it might be a little too close to that spot," Lena said, watching me out of the corner of her eye.

I just shrugged and smiled.

We didn't stay long at the second apartment either. It was a one-bedroom on the first floor. Phyllis, the current tenant, was there. She had lived in the apartment for the last thirty years, but now she was moving into the nursing home. Her light blue sweater matched her eyes, and she kept her white hair in a low bun. When she smiled, the number of wrinkles on her face doubled. She was there because she wanted to give me a heads up about a few "quirks". Like apparently the hot water went out every couple of weeks. "There's something really refreshing about taking a cold shower," Phyllis said, to my look of disbelief. "And you're just going to love Luther," she said.

"Who's Luther?"

"He lives upstairs, and he is the most talented tap dancer I've ever seen. He works the late shift at the diner, so he usually starts practicing around midnight. He's really dedicated too. He practices for two or three hours. And it's so funny, his dog will howl the entire time he's dancing. I think he's singing along. I just love listening to them," she said. I had backed out the door before she was even finished talking.

"Thanks, Phyllis. Good luck with the move," Lena said. "So, we'll put that on the maybe list?" Lena asked with a sly smile as we walked down the street.

The third apartment was the one on Sparkle Street. I simultaneously loved and hated the name. On the one hand, it was adorable. On the other hand, I was embarrassed at the thought of giving directions. "Turn left on Sparkle Street. It's the third shimmering building on your right."

The building was actually brick. It was right next to the grocery store, Basil's Market, where Holly and her mom,

Luanne, worked. The apartment was on the third floor. It was a studio in the corner of the building so two of the walls had fairly large windows. The kitchen was tiny, but, outside of the pie shop, I didn't really do a lot of cooking anyway. The appliances were a mint green as though straight out of the sixties. I liked the retro vibe. It had creaky dark wood floors, and the bathroom was almost as big as the rest of the apartment with a giant walk-in shower.

"Have you seen this shower?" I asked Lena as I stood in the middle of it and marveled at the two shower heads. The bathroom had white and black checkered tiles, which could be a lot to process in the morning, but I liked it.

"I was saving the best for last," she said. "This one is available right away, and the landlord is willing to do a month-to-month lease so you don't even have to commit for a whole year."

There was really no reason for me not to do it. "This is the place," I said with a decisive nod. Soon Henry and I could have a little alone time. I smiled at the thought.

"What are you thinking about?" Lena asked when she noticed my smile.

"Nothing," I said, blushing.

"Uh huh," she said knowingly.

When I got back to the pie shop, I jumped right in serving customers so I didn't have to answer any questions about where I'd been. On the flip side, I didn't have a chance to press Aunt Erma more about the voicemail. She and I were never alone, and she conveniently left to run an errand just as we were getting ready to close. Something strange was going on, and I wanted to get to the bottom of it. My mom said she could finish up the prep for tomorrow and sent me upstairs to get ready to go to the ice show.

The dogs were excited to see me. I took them outside and when we got back Mitzy busied herself trying to squeak her stuffed pig to death. Duncan grabbed the pig from her and rested his head on it. Having another dog in the apartment really could come in handy.

I wandered around for a few minutes. Something just seemed off with Aunt Erma. What if she was still under a spell? I didn't know what I was looking for. I picked up pieces of paper and looked behind picture frames. Duncan stood up and walked over to the table where Aunt Erma still had piles of pictures sitting out. She had put her sorting project on hold once the spell was broken.

"Is there something here?" I asked, looking down at the pictures. His tail wagged harder. Mitzy began to growl behind Duncan. Duncan turned and gave her one bark, and Mitzy stopped, but kept glaring at us. Duncan skillfully ignored Mitzy's gaze.

I picked up one pile. It was mostly pictures of the Morning Pie Crew dressed up in costumes. I assumed it was for Halloween, but with this crowd I couldn't be sure. The next stack was mostly pictures of Mitzy as a puppy.

"Mitzy, you were so adorable," I said.

She stuck her nose in the air as though to say, "What do you mean 'were'?"

I grabbed a handful of the pictures that were still in the box. She hadn't sorted these yet. I was in some of them. I ached when I looked at a picture of my parents, Aunt Erma, and me huddled around a cake on my sixth birthday. I had wanted a cake shaped like a pony. Aunt Erma and my mother had baked me a pony cake, and my father had frosted it. It was beautiful, and to this day I remembered it as being the most delicious cake I'd ever eaten.

I flipped to the next picture. It was a snapshot of Aunt Erma with her arms around some man. I studied it closer. The man's mouth was smiling, but his eyes were sharp. I hadn't ever seen him before, but the two of them sure looked cozy.

"Who is this?" I asked Mitzy. Mitzy went over to the corner and lay down in her bed with her back to me.

In the picture, Aunt Erma was wearing a green teardrop necklace. I had seen that necklace somewhere before.

I pulled out my phone and snapped a picture of the photo. Aunt Erma might have the sudden urge to tidy up this project, and I couldn't risk the photo disappearing before I found out why it was important.

I glanced at the clock. I had to go meet Henry. I put on three pairs of fleece-lined leggings, a tank top and two long-sleeve shirts, a heavy gray sweater, my red coat with a green scarf, and a red hat. I put on a pair of regular socks and then a pair of wool socks over those and shoved my feet into my boots. I topped off the look with both gloves and my green mittens just to be safe.

The ice show was at the outdoor ice rink where Henry and I had our first pre-date just a few weeks ago. Henry and I had played hockey. I'd won the game by a landslide, and he'd had to buy drinks at Sal's afterward. I had to admit I was a little excited to go back to the scene where sparks had first flown between us.

The ice rink was even more beautiful than I remembered it. There were still Christmas lights hanging on the trees that surrounded the clearing. They had hung even more twinkling lights on poles around the ice rink and had brought in spotlights and bleachers. It was really a nice set up. It, of course, would have been even nicer if it were about fifty degrees warmer outside.

People were already gathering and buying their tickets and hot chocolate from Wally, the hot-chocolate guy. I hoped that the night would be all about watching ice skating and not about saving everyone from evil magic. Violet was still trying to minimize the problem so people in town wouldn't panic. I wasn't sure if that was the right thing to do or not, but I was too new in town to disagree with her.

"Hey, you." I heard Henry's voice behind me. I gave him a hug.

"If these kids aren't good, we can go out there and show them how it's done," I joked.

A woman passing by shot me an evil glare. Clearly her child was one of the skaters. "Just kidding," I called after her. "Geez, these skating parents are intense," I said to Henry.

"You have no idea," he said, shaking his head. He lowered his voice and leaned in. "I heard that several parents were kicked out of ice-show rehearsals for getting too involved."

I would have to try to keep my hilarious comments to myself. I was afraid of incurring the wrath of a skating parent almost as much as I was afraid of the IMPs. We bought our tickets and a couple of paper cups of hot chocolate.

"Can I buy a couple more of these to pour over my body?" I asked Henry, holding up my steaming cup. He raised his eyebrows. "Wait, that came out wrong," I said, laughing. I got another glare from a man sitting in front of us.

"There are children around," he said sharply.

"Sorry," I said. "I just meant I was cold. Maybe I should buy a couple cups for you to pour on your soul." I smiled and took a sip of my hot chocolate.

"You are going to keep everyone on their toes, aren't you?" Henry asked. I shrugged innocently.

The lights in the crowd dimmed and spotlights lit the ice. A Christmas medley played and the whole cast came out wearing red outfits trimmed in white fur. I became so absorbed in their performance, I almost forgot we were watching out for the IMPs.

I scanned the crowd looking for someone or something amiss. When I glanced over at Henry, I could tell he was watching everything all at once without looking as if he was watching everything. He was almost too good at this. I wondered how many stakeouts he'd been on in his life. Was this a regular thing in this magical town?

I wanted to ask him, but the last thing I needed was Mr. Frigid in front of us glaring at me again, so I just examined the crowd some more. The advanced skaters were on the ice now, doing jumps and spins I had only ever dreamed about doing. I had three years of ice-skating lessons under my belt but my commitment to the sport had faltered when I'd realized that falling hurt, and it would only get worse the higher I jumped.

I saw movement out of the corner of my eye and turned my head. It was him. The man from Aunt Erma's picture. At least I think it was. The spotlight swept across his face, and I was sure. He was older, but he had the same sharp eyes. I leapt out of my seat.

"What are you ...?" Henry began to ask, but I was hurrying down the bleachers.

"Hey," a couple people called as I bumped them on my way down. I hated bleachers. They were really hard to escape from in a timely manner. And Henry and I had sat near the back so that we would have a good view of the whole crowd.

I made eye contact with the man for only a second, and he hurried away. I rushed after him. I was trying to run discreetly, which wasn't easy. I was getting closer. I was almost close enough to tap him on the shoulder of his tan coat.

"Excuse me," I tried, but he didn't turn around. Suddenly my feet weren't under me anymore. I was airborne for a second. It would have been fun if I hadn't known what was coming next. I landed hard. I heard a crack.

"Are you okay?" A group of people surrounded me.

"Yup," I lied, but I didn't get up. Pain was shooting through my foot.

Henry crouched down next to me within seconds. "Are you okay?"

"I fell on the triple axel," I said with a slight groan. I contemplated standing up. "I think we should go." The crowd was still watching me. I grabbed Henry's hand, and a couple other people were quick to help me up. I drew my breath in sharply when I put weight on my right foot. Yup, that hurt. People were staring, and I didn't want to make any more of a scene than I already had.

"Please, get me out of here," I whispered, holding tightly onto Henry's arm. He murmured some words, and I felt my body become lighter. It didn't hurt as much, and I was able to walk out of there.

"Did you see something?" he asked in a low voice.

"Not exactly," I said.

Once we were out of the crowd, he picked me up and carried me. "This would be really romantic if I didn't feel like a total klutz," I said. I explained about the man from the picture. "I don't know who he is, but I feel like there's something going on with Aunt Erma, and I need to figure it out. This guy is a missing piece of the puzzle."

I showed him the picture on my phone, but he didn't know who the man was.

"Hopefully it will all become clear soon. Erma is a powerful woman. She probably knows lots of people, and, to be honest, she's just kind of a strange person. She's entitled to a little kookiness with all that she goes through," he said. "And you're entitled to a little kookiness too."

Henry got me back to the pie shop and put me down in a chair out front. My mother was gone, but Aunt Erma was there. Holly appeared at the door seconds after we arrived.

"What did you do to her?" she demanded of Henry, pointing at me.

Henry held his hands up. "This was all her doing. She fell doing her triple axel."

"Have you gone to the doctor?" she asked.

"No, that's not necessary," I said. The swelling was pushing on my boot, and the pain wasn't going away. "I probably just need to ice it."

Aunt Erma bent down at my feet. She very gently touched my foot. I felt guilty for thinking that she could be up to something.

"I think it's broken. We should probably take her to see Dr. Gabel," she said.

"Can't you just magic it better?" I asked.

"No, healing magic can be tricky, especially with bones. If you do it wrong, it can be really hard to fix," Henry said. "Sorry, gimpy."

The doctor confirmed my fear that I'd broken my foot. He prescribed ice, rest, and a very stylish gray walking cast.

Chapter 15

Dear Elodie,

    I recently got into a fight with my best friend. He borrowed a couple of books months ago. Since then, I've asked if I could have the books back several times, but he keeps putting off returning them. I finally snapped. It was one of those perfect storm arguments that starts about nothing and then explodes with both sides saying hurtful things they shouldn't.

    I have since apologized for the things I said. I told him I would still really like the books back. He said he forgave me, but he hasn't returned the books, and he hasn't apologized for the terrible things he said.

    I find myself turning down his invitations to hang out or dodging his phone calls. How can we fix this bump in our friendship? And how do I get my books back?

Sincerely,
Forgive or Fume?

Dear Forgive or Fume?

My question to you is why do you want to fix this friendship? From what you've said, this guy is dismissive about your feelings and your possessions. Talk to him about your argument, and address the things he said that hurt you. Sometimes people are blind to their own mistakes, and he may honestly not recognize that he owes you an apology too. If he still ignores your concerns, it might be time to cut ties and search for healthier relationships.

As for the books, my mother always told me you should never lend out something you want back. My guess is that he lost the books, but a best friend should own up to that and offer to replace them.

Ask and I'll Answer,

Elodie

Violet assigned me security camera duty. I was supposed to sit, watch the screen, and call her if I saw Dennis, Brenda, or Stan, or anything that looked suspicious. "How did this happen?" she asked when she came over to drop off the computer I needed to watch security cameras.

"I slipped." I shrugged, but I couldn't look her in the eye. She had laser eyes that I was pretty sure would be able to see the truth if I looked into them.

I set up at a table in the front of the pie shop with my foot wrapped in an ice pack and propped up on a chair. My back was against the wall so none of the customers who came in would be able to see the screen. Not that it really mattered if they could anyway. It was pretty boring stuff.

I could see kids having a snowball fight outside of a school. A bicyclist was locking up her bike. Several people were walking down streets with shopping bags. A paper cup was blowing in the wind. A few people had taken their dogs out to relieve themselves. I saw one man walking down the street with his untied shoelace flopping on the ground. It was an accident waiting to happen, but I was pretty sure Violet didn't want me to call and tell her about it. I watched the cycling security footage intently at first. No IMP activity would go unnoticed on my watch.

My mother was at the pie shop again today. It was good she was still in town since I was much less helpful now. Despite my weakened state, she still managed to work in three passive-aggressive comments and two outright insults about my outfit. She did, however, also serve me coffee along with her insults, so glass half full.

After about twenty minutes, I was wishing that I could watch some soap operas or something instead of just security camera footage. I stared blankly at the screen. Focus, Susie, I tried to tell myself, and I shifted in my seat. I might need a lot of coffee to get through this.

I got up a couple times to serve customers, but I was more of a hindrance than a help. I dropped forks and served upside down slices of pie because balancing on one foot and scooping pie was difficult. The doctor told me I could put weight on my broken foot, but it hurt every time I tried. I wanted to break her foot and see if she could put weight on it.

Henry stopped by a little after noon. "I come bearing sustenance," he said, holding out a large brown paper bag.

"Tacos and nachos," I said, peering into the bag. "You really are the perfect man."

"There's enough in there for your mom and Erma too," he said. "Unless you're really hungry, and then they never have to know."

"Hey, I heard that," Aunt Erma yelled from the kitchen.

"Please tell me you have some time to hang out." I pulled him down into the chair next to me.

"For you, always," he said. He updated me on everything that was happening at the nursing home while we shared the nachos. There was a little holiday romance happening between Frank and Claire. Henry had overheard Frank asking around trying to get Claire's name in the Secret Santa exchange.

My phone rang, and I answered without checking the caller ID.

"Susie, it's Buster Hopkins from Top-Notch Construction. I was just calling to see if you've considered my job offer. We'd really like you to start after the holidays."

"I really appreciate the offer," I said. I glanced at Henry. He was watching me intently. "I think I'm going to have to say—"

Buster interrupted before I could finish. "You hold onto that thought. I want you to think about it for a few more days. I think I can even get you a little more paid vacation time than we talked about last time. Talk to you later." He hung up.

"You got a job offer?" he asked.

"Yeah, from a company in the city. I don't plan on taking it though." I studied the computer screen.

"Why didn't you tell me?"

"I didn't think it was a big deal." I shrugged.

"Or maybe you were thinking about taking it?" It was part statement, part question.

I didn't respond fast enough, and he stood up. "I have to get back to work," he said.

Just then, Josh walked in. He gave Henry a little wave. Henry narrowed his eyes at him and left. I saw my mother peeking around the corner from the kitchen with an amused look on her face. I was glad my personal struggles were entertaining her.

Josh came over and sat down across from me.

"I heard you were hobbling around, so I brought food." He set a bag down in front of me. He'd picked up some sandwiches from the diner, including my favorite grilled cheese.

"Thank you," I said.

He noticed the bag of tacos and cringed. "You've already eaten?"

"Yes."

231

"Never mind, I should have known." He grabbed the bag off the table.

"It was really sweet. Thank you." I snatched the bag from his hand. My stomach felt as if it were going to burst after the nachos, but I unwrapped the sandwich and took a small bite.

I told him the edited version about my fall. I left out the fact that I was chasing a man I'd recognized from one of Aunt Erma's photos.

My mother came out to talk to Josh, and, within the first ten seconds of the conversation, she managed to work in the fact that I'd gotten a job offer from Top-Notch Construction.

Josh's eyes lit up. I was going to tell them both that I wasn't planning on taking the job, but the two of them went off on a conversation about my future that didn't seem to require any input from me. I stopped paying much attention and started watching the camera feed on the computer again.

Then I saw him with his slicked back hair. I tried to zoom in on the picture, but it was grainy. I was pretty sure it was him. The guy from Aunt Erma's photo. The tag on the corner of the security camera said he was in the next town over. He paused on the sidewalk, looked both ways, and then crossed the street and went through the door of a coffee shop.

My mother got up to serve some customers. I put my walking cast on.

"Where are you going? I'll come with you," Josh offered.

I closed the computer and stood up. "No need," I said. "We'll catch up later."

I mouthed to my mom that I would be back soon, and I limped out the door without looking back. Josh followed me out.

"How are you going to drive?" he asked. He pointed at my right foot.

He had a point. I hadn't thought about that. I probably couldn't push the pedals. At least not safely. I would just have to come up with a plan to get him out of the coffee shop once we got there.

"Sure, if you wouldn't mind, that would be great. Thanks," I said.

"So where are we going and why can't we tell your family?" he asked. I had almost forgotten how well he knew me.

"I have this meeting at a coffee shop," I said. My mind was racing. "I'm going for an interview. I don't want Aunt Erma to know because, you know, awkward."

He nodded. "Sure. Is the family time too much?"

"Yes," I said, but I could feel that it was forced. I felt disloyal to Aunt Erma for even saying the words.

The drive was nice. We caught up on everything that was happening back home. I promised I would return to the job site to finish hanging the light fixtures. He told me it wasn't necessary because the electrician had arrived and taken care of it. I felt a twinge of disappointment, but realized, with everything going on, it was probably for the best. I was beginning to relax and not think about how he had proclaimed his love or how I was on my way to meet a man I didn't know.

"Can we get back to our earlier conversation?" he asked the moment there was a lull. We were at a stoplight, and he turned to look at me. His eyes gazed intently.

How did I let a lull happen? I should have kept talking. I should have asked him questions about everyone we'd ever met just to keep this conversation from happening.

"I really should focus on my interview," I said. "We're almost there."

He sighed and turned his eyes back to the road.

Chapter 16

Dear Elodie,

I'm at a crossroads in my life. One of those truly big life-changing moments. The problem is I can't decide which path to take. Left or right, my life will be completely different. How do I make this major decision?

Sincerely,
Wondering Which Way

Dear Wondering Which Way,

I could go on and on about making pro con lists or doing research, but the truth is you should follow your heart.

Ask and I'll Answer,

Elodie

I sat in the truck for a minute after we pulled into a parking spot. We could just turn around and go back to the pie shop. Maybe I wasn't supposed to find out Aunt

Erma's secret. Maybe there wasn't even a secret to find out. There could be a perfectly logical explanation for the strange voicemail, Aunt Erma's odd behavior, and this man from the photo who was suddenly lurking around. All this IMP stuff had me on high alert, and maybe I was creating drama where there wasn't any.

Josh was watching me. "Remember to mention all the marketing you did at Hal's during that holiday promotion," he said.

"Right, the 'Give the gift of straight shelves' campaign," I said with a laugh. "Everyone loves shelves, but most people hate to hang them. Don't hesitate to call Hal's Handyman Services." I gave him an overly enthusiastic thumbs-up after running through part of the commercial I'd written for Hal. I had told Josh I was interviewing for a marketing job. It was the first thing that had come to mind.

"You're going to be great in there," he said.

"Thanks." I opened the car door. Josh got out too. I froze. "I can't bring a buddy to an interview," I said.

"I'll sit at a different table. You won't even know I'm here. I just want to make sure you don't slip on your way in," he said. I finally agreed because the more I fought it, the more suspicious he was getting.

"Just sit far away so you don't make me nervous," I said.

I held my breath as Josh held the door. I scanned the faces in the shop. It was one of those large warehouse spaces with cement floors and exposed beams in the ceiling.

There were two large wooden tables and several smaller ones where people were working on their laptops.

He was still there. Sitting at a small table in the back corner, staring at his phone, was the man from the picture.

"Do you want a cup of coffee?" Josh asked.

I shook my head. The last thing I needed was coffee. I was already feeling anxious and jittery. He nodded and went to the counter to order himself a cup.

I approached the table. The man's white hair was slicked back, and I could see streaks of the dark brown hair that he'd had in the picture. His bushy gray eyebrows were pinched together as he typed furiously on his phone. He wore the same tan coat he'd had on at the ice show. He hadn't taken it off even though it was plenty warm in here. I stood over him until he looked up. He looked annoyed for a minute before recognition swept over his face.

"You look like her, you know," he said, then studied me as though debating his next move. I had him pinned in the corner. His only way out would be to push me down. "Sit." He nodded to the chair across from him.

I sat. I really wished I had prepared better for this meeting. I shouldn't have been chatting so much in the car. I pulled out my phone where I had the picture of the photograph of Aunt Erma and this man.

"Is this you?" I asked. It was obvious it was. Unless he was going to pull the "I have an evil twin" thing.

He nodded.

"How do you know my aunt?"

"Don't you know who I am?" he asked. He said it in a way that made me really wish I did know who he was. I shook my head. I took a moment to glance over and make sure Josh wasn't sitting anywhere near us. He was at a table across the room playing on his phone and drinking a large cup of coffee.

Great. Josh could never handle his caffeine. I would be barraged with show tunes the whole drive back. Or worse, his impersonations of actors, musicians, and talk-show hosts. He would go on and on and there was no stopping him when he had too much coffee in his system.

"Who are you? Do you know Dennis and Brenda? Or Stan?" I asked.

He took a deep breath. He was interrupted by a pitch pipe. A group by the front door began singing "Deck the Halls". They were wearing Santa hats and red capes. I'd forgotten we were still in a small town and things like this happened. They were loud carolers, and we had to pause our discussion for a minute. Finally, they finished. I joined in the applause, but the man sitting across from me did not. He just stared into his coffee cup until it was all over.

"I'm Ivan Price," he said once the noise died down. He seemed to be looking for a reaction.

"How do you know my aunt?"

"Erma and I were ..." he paused for a second "... *close*, for a while."

I didn't like the way he said "close".

"That was almost twenty years ago. We were doing some amazing things back then. Making real changes. I've been trying to get a hold of her, but she seems to be dodging me."

"Maybe you should leave her alone," I said.

"It's not like everything that's been happening to Erma is completely unwarranted," Ivan said.

"What do you mean?" I was instantly defensive.

He laughed, which made me even more angry. "You don't know that much about Erma, do you?"

My face felt hot, and I wondered if I could spill his coffee on him without making a big scene.

"She hasn't always been the good fairy of Hocus Hills, you know," he said. "Her magic hasn't always been so innocent. Why do you think everyone is after her?"

I'd always thought it was because she was so powerful.

"We want her back on our side. We could make major strides improving the lives of magical people if she came back to our side and quit hiding at her pie shop."

My head was spinning. Was he just trying to mess with me? Aunt Erma had never been involved with the IMPs. She definitely would have told me in one of our drunken late-night chat sessions. Definitely, I told myself.

"You're lying." I tried to keep my voice from wavering.

He took a smug sip of his coffee.

"Hasn't she been acting strangely lately?" he asked.

"No," I lied.

"Let me see that picture again," he said. I pulled it up

on my phone and showed it to him. "See that necklace she's wearing?" I looked at the green teardrop necklace. "All the IMPs wear them. It was actually Erma's idea. They connect us." He reached under his white button-up shirt and pulled out an identical necklace to the one in the picture. It was the same one Sally had been wearing in her shop. Sally was an IMP too? The necklace had a sinister glow, and I leaned back in my chair. Then it hit me. I knew where else I'd seen that necklace. Nellie had been wearing the same one.

"So you're one of them." I couldn't keep the disgust out of my tone.

"One of them?" He laughed. "I'm not just one of them. I started the movement. Well, with Erma's help. I'm Ivan Michael Price, founder of the Improvement for Magical People."

I realized my mouth was hanging open, so I closed it.

"I know you're new here, but you belong with us. So does Erma."

"My aunt wants to *stop* the IMPs," I said. I was clutching my phone tightly.

"Are you sure about that?"

"Why are you starting trouble now?"

"I wouldn't call it trouble." He dismissed me so calmly. I tried to slow my breath, which was now coming out in short angry bursts. "Things kind of died down after Erma left. People lost interest without the promise of her power, but people are getting tired of hiding. We're picking up steam again. We're going to take over with or without Erma. We just need the secret to her power."

For the first time, I felt as if I might actually be in danger. I didn't want Ivan to try and get Aunt Erma's secret out of me. What if he put a truth spell on me?

I glanced across the room to check on Josh again. He wasn't at his table. Instead he was looking through a stack of newspapers at a table not too far away from where I was sitting. How long had he been there? Could he hear what we were talking about? We had to get out of here.

I stood up quickly. "Nice to meet you, Mr. Price," I said loudly. Ivan made a move to stand up. "No," I said sharply. He fell back in his chair as though I'd knocked him over. His eyes were wide for a second, then he smiled slightly.

"I see you take after your aunt," he said.

I didn't give him the chance to say anything else. I hurried out the door as fast as my walking cast would take me. I was halfway back to the car before Josh caught up to me.

"Hey." He gently grabbed my arm as he caught up to me. "Are you okay?"

"Of course," I said, flashing him a smile, but I could feel the smile waver a little. I struggled to keep my balance on an icy patch on the sidewalk.

"How'd it go?" He looked as if he wanted to offer his hand to help steady me. I folded my arms across my chest.

"Fine."

He began humming the song "Maybe" from *Annie* and

I braced myself for the full-on singing outburst. It didn't come, though. "I was definitely not trying to listen in," Josh said when we got into the truck. "But I may have overheard a thing or two, and it sounded like you guys were having a weird conversation. What is that? Some new kind of interviewing technique?"

"He was a strange guy," I said. "Apparently everyone in the company wears matching necklaces, and he kept going on and on about how they try to create magic wherever they go. A little too hippy dippy for me."

He started the truck. "So, what's the plan, then?"

"I think I'm going to stay at the pie shop for a while." I looked out the window, so I didn't have to look at his face. I was silent for a minute. "I got an apartment in Hocus Hills."

He let out a long slow breath. "Is this your way of saying you don't love me back?"

"I don't love you like you want me to. I love you like a best friend," I said. I saw his fingers tighten around the steering wheel. I wished that we weren't having this conversation in a car like this. I wanted to give him a hug. Instead I watched the car in front of us too.

"We're so good together," he said.

"But we've never been on the same page at the same time. It shouldn't be that hard," I said. We pulled into a parking spot near the pie shop. Josh turned off the engine and looked down at the keys in his hand. I reached out and gently touched his arm. He didn't move. "We've always been better suited as friends. I've missed you, but I've been selfish leading you on because I like your company."

"You've always been selfish," he said. He got out of the truck, shut the door hard, and walked away.

I sat there frozen for a minute. My heart was pounding. I tried not to cry. I didn't want to start, but once the first tear was out, there was no stopping the rest from following. That was the problem with crying. It released all the emotions that had been carefully caged. I cried for Josh. I cried for Aunt Erma and the years we weren't together and the things she might have done. I cried for another Christmas without my dad.

There was a tap at the window. Darn these small towns. I wiped my face on the sleeve of my coat and looked over to see Henry's concerned face peering in at me. I tried to pull myself together as I opened the door, but instead a fresh wave of tears came. He didn't ask me what was wrong, he just wrapped me in his arms and let me cry.

Chapter 17

Dear Elodie,

Last week I gave a friend/co-worker of mine flowers for her birthday while we were at work. The next day I saw the same flowers in the dumpster. When I asked her about it, she said she felt uncomfortable displaying flowers from me. I wasn't trying to make any major proclamation. I just wanted to get her something to brighten her day. I can't help but feel hurt, and I'm not sure how to talk to her about it. Any advice would be appreciated.

Sincerely,
Friend Flower Fail

Dear Friend Flower Fail,

Try something like this – "I just wanted to get you something to brighten your day. I'm sorry if I made you uncomfortable." In the future maybe just pitch

in on an office present or sign the office card to avoid
putting anyone in an uncomfortable situation.
   Ask and I'll Answer,

Elodie

My meltdown didn't last too long. I had questions to ask Aunt Erma. I pulled away from Henry and started laughing.

"What?" He looked alarmed, as if I might have actually fallen off my rocker this time. He was twisted awkwardly so he could hug me.

"How are you holding that position?" I asked in a tearful giggle.

"I sneak into yoga sometimes," he said. He straightened up with a slight groan. "Maybe I should sneak into some more classes." He pulled a handkerchief out of his pocket, because, apparently, he was a gentleman from the eighteen hundreds. I wiped my face and blew my nose.

"Here," I said with a wicked smile as I handed him the dirty handkerchief back.

"Thanks." To my surprise he took it and put it back in his pocket. I was simultaneously touched and repulsed.

I told Henry about my conversation with Josh. He remained silent while I talked. Occasionally his face would twitch as though his emotions were threatening to burst out. When I finished my story, he somehow managed to look angry, sympathetic, and relieved all at the same time.

"You are the least selfish person I know. He shouldn't

have said that to you. But if he feels even a fraction of what I feel for you, I can imagine how awful he must have felt when you told him you don't feel the same way," Henry said. "But that doesn't excuse his behavior," he added quickly.

"I just hope Josh and I can be friends again someday," I said.

"I hope you can too." Henry gave me another squeeze. I couldn't tell if he meant it, but I appreciated the sentiment.

"Where have you been?" my mother asked the moment we walked through the door. When she noticed I'd been crying she asked, "What's wrong?" Then she turned sharply to Henry. "What did you do to her?"

"It's nothing, Mom. My foot just hurts a little," I said. "I was out running some errands. I was a little too ambitious about how far I could walk in this thing." I pointed to the walking cast on my foot. "Henry helped me back." This would all probably come out as a lie at some point. I'm sure someone in town saw me in the truck with Josh, and probably at least one person saw me crying on Henry's shoulder from their window. I would deal with that later.

"I have to go get ready for Frank's big outing," Henry said. He studied my face, his brow furrowed. "Are you okay?"

"Absolutely." I smiled brightly. "I'll meet you at the nursing home soon."

"It's okay if you don't want to go anymore." He gently squeezed my hand.

"Susie, I don't think you should go out again if your foot hurts," my mother said.

"I'll be fine," I said. Nothing was going to keep me from this.

She "tsked" loudly and walked away, shaking her head.

When I arrived at Enchanted Woods it was clear everyone inside was ready to burst with the excitement of keeping a secret for too long. By some miracle it appeared that Henry had managed to keep the day's activities a surprise from Frank.

Frank looked around at everyone as though studying who might spill the beans first.

"Are you ready?" Henry asked him.

"Son, I'm always ready for anything!"

With that, the crew shuffled outside to the bus. I had been telling Henry for weeks that they needed a new bus. This one was rusty and creaky and the seats were so worn you could feel every spring when you sat down. Apparently this was the bus they'd taken to a Rod Stewart concert a few years ago, and when they were getting back on the bus at the end of the concert, Rod had stopped to help Bernie after she'd tripped. There was some speculation that her trip had been staged, but she denied it to this day. However, in the process of helping her, Rod had touched the side of the bus. Now they were determined to ride the Rod-mobile forever.

"Isn't this exciting?" Claire whispered to me. Though, to be honest, her whisper wasn't much quieter than her regular voice.

I smiled and nodded, afraid if I gave her too much encouragement, she would spoil the surprise.

"What do you think of Frank?" she asked.

"He seems like a very nice man," I said.

"He's got a cute butt, doesn't he?" she asked.

I carefully studied the frost on the window and desperately tried not to think about Frank's butt.

"Stop embarrassing the girl," Sandy chimed in from the seat behind us.

"I was just looking for her opinion." She held her hands up defensively.

Luckily the drive to the hill at the edge of town was short and soon everyone was shuffling off the bus again.

The look on Frank's face when he saw the bobsled was truly priceless. I felt a lump at the back of my throat and looked over at Henry. He was blinking a lot.

Upon closer examination I saw that Henry had pretty thoroughly padded the inside of the sled, probably hoping to avoid any injuries. He'd told me he'd put a protection spell on it too. The side of the hill we were on was tall, but the slope was gentle and clear of trees and rocks. Henry had solicited the help of some people in town to build a bobsled track out of snow.

"All right, now I need you to be careful," Henry was telling Frank as he handed him a helmet.

"Yeah yeah." Frank waved him away. He turned to Claire. "Would you like to go with me, darling?"

"That would be swell," she said. They both put on their helmets and Henry helped them into the sled.

"Super careful," Henry warned one more time and they were off.

The crowd of residents cheered their departure. Frank threw his hands up in the air as the sled made its way down the hill, riding up on curves and over dips.

"Woohoo," I heard him yell.

"Woohoo," Claire echoed.

Henry shook his head, but smiled.

Bernie breezed past me. "Remember to let the chopsticks fall."

"Thanks, Bernie." I still didn't know what it meant.

"What was that about?" Henry asked.

I shrugged.

"Do you think they'll get together?" I pointed to the bobsled as it veered around another corner.

"I don't know. Claire has always liked to keep her options open, but they do seem to have a spark." He watched them nearing the bottom. "I better go pick them up. Can you stay here with everyone?"

"Absolutely."

My nosiness was getting the best of me. As he left, I casually reached up to my ear and murmured the spell Bernie had taught me. I looked down at Claire and Frank. They'd slowed to a stop at the bottom of the hill, but they hadn't moved from the sled. The spell worked and I could hear them breathing hard.

"I'm glad I got to share this experience with you," Frank said.

"Kiss me, hot stuff," Claire said.

I quickly turned away. I'd heard enough. My gaze turned to Sandy and Candace, who were standing a little ways away from the rest of the group. It looked as if they were having an intense conversation.

"... thinks they're onto something." I tuned in in the middle of Sandy's sentence.

"I heard they almost had her," Candace said. "If they get her, I'm definitely in."

"I never thought we should be hiding. And I'm old now. What do I have to lose?" Sandy said.

Just then the creaky bus pulled back up to the top of the hill, and everyone's attention turned to the returning bobsledders. Frank's eyes were bright and his smile stretched ear to ear. He looked like a little kid bouncing around.

Frank took several more rides down the hill with the few other willing passengers.

After we dropped all the residents back at the nursing home, Henry walked me back to the pie shop. Violet and my mother were having a whispered conversation when we walked in.

"Is everything okay?" Henry asked Violet.

"Have either of you seen Erma lately?"

We both shook our heads. "Not since this morning. Why?" I asked.

"There's been some chatter that the IMPs are going to try something big. I came to warn Erma, but when I got here, your mother said she'd stepped out for a minute," Violet said.

"She's not answering her cell phone, and we're afraid they got to her," my mother said.

I had a sinking feeling in my stomach. Or maybe she went back to their side. I wasn't sure if I should tell Violet and my mother what I'd learned from Ivan. I decided against it. She was still my aunt, after all, and if she hadn't gone to join the IMPs, I would be tarnishing her reputation for no reason.

Violet decided she needed to call in the Morning Pie Crew.

"I need their help searching for Erma, but we need to keep a low profile," she said. "We don't want the rest of the town to realize how dire the situation is. A bunch of magical people panicking would just make this all even more dangerous."

I had an idea where Aunt Erma might be, but I had to get out of the pie shop without raising suspicions.

Flora, Lena, and Mr. Barnes got to the pie shop quickly. Violet filled them in while my mother called Aunt Erma's cell phone repeatedly. I told her that Aunt Erma often forgot to turn on her cell phone or left it in the car, but my mother kept trying anyway. Not that I blamed her. It was strange for Aunt Erma to be gone so long on one of our busy days before the holiday. It was even stranger that no one had seen her during that time.

Henry helped me serve any customers that came in. Some people looked over at the group huddled around the table with raised eyebrows. "They're planning a Christmas surprise," I would say with a bright smile, and everyone seemed to accept that explanation.

The Morning Pie Crew left to go on their mission to find Aunt Erma. Violet gave my mother and I strict instructions to stay at the pie shop in case Aunt Erma came back. Plus, we had to make sure everything appeared as normal as possible to the townspeople.

"Of course, we'll stay here," I assured Violet. But in my head, I was thinking, Fat chance. She nodded, satisfied, and left.

As though on cue, the dogs started barking upstairs. "I'd better take them on a walk," I told my mother.

"I'll help," Henry offered and followed me upstairs.

Mitzy danced around our feet, and Duncan was on the sofa under my blanket with his head on my pillow.

"Hey, get off of there," I scolded. "You have a dog bed for a reason." He reluctantly dragged himself off the sofa.

"Do you trust me?" I asked Henry.

"Of course," he said.

"I need to go out for a little bit. I can't tell you where I'm going. Can you cover for me?"

"Are you going to do something dangerous?" he asked.

I hesitated. "Hopefully not too dangerous." There was the part of me that desperately wanted Henry to come along, but I still felt as if I had to keep the tree a secret. What if Aunt Erma really was just out doing some Christmas shopping or something? What if the IMPs had no idea there even was a magic tree? I couldn't burden him with this secret and betray Aunt Erma's trust until I knew more.

"Can you at least take Duncan with you? I'd feel better if you had a guard dog along," he said.

I looked over at Duncan. He let out a gigantic yawn and blinked sleepily at us. "Him? You'd feel better if I had him along?" I asked.

Henry smiled. "Yes."

"Fine, I'll bring him along."

"Can you drive with that thing?" He nodded to my walking cast.

"I'll find a way," I said confidently.

"Okay. Call me if you need anything," he said. He held my gaze for a minute and then we kissed. I hoped he couldn't hear my anxious heart pounding in my chest.

I said goodbye and left with Duncan sluggishly following me. He seemed happy to discover we were going on a car ride, not a walk.

I took the walking cast off when we got to the car. It hurt to press the pedals, but it wasn't unbearable. I cranked up the Christmas music to distract myself from the pain. Duncan watched out the window for a few minutes, but soon he was sprawled across the back seat snoring loudly. "You're supposed to provide protection," I reminded him, but he didn't wake up.

As we drove, I wondered if Aunt Erma would have really brought the IMPs to the magic tree. I hoped I was about to prove all of my suspicions wrong. I turned down the dirt road, and I saw her car parked off to the side. This wasn't where the tree was. I parked a little ways away, though it was hard to hide on this deserted road. Duncan perked up when the car stopped. He leapt over the front seat and out the door in case I was thinking about leaving him behind.

There were multiple sets of footprints in the snow starting at Aunt Erma's car. We followed them. Duncan grabbed the corner of my coat with his teeth. I was about to scold him when I heard voices.

"I think I'm all turned around." It was Aunt Erma.

"Stan followed your niece out to these woods. We know your magic comes from something in here," a woman's voice said. It sounded like Brenda.

"Yes, and I want to share it with you. I think I turned at the wrong rock," Aunt Erma said.

I caught a glimpse of them and quickly sidestepped behind a tree. Duncan pressed up against my leg.

Ivan grabbed Aunt Erma's arm and pulled her away from the group. Brenda marched off making snide comments about Aunt Erma's magic fading as she aged. Dennis and Stan reluctantly slinked off behind her.

"For goodness sake, we're the same age, Brenda," Aunt Erma yelled after her. She shook her head in disgust.

Ivan stepped closer to Aunt Erma. "I wasn't sure we'd get you back," he said softly. I had to hold my breath to listen.

"Of course," she said. "I was just waiting for the right time."

My heart stopped.

He touched her face.

"You're cold," he said. He pulled a gray and blue knitted scarf out from under his coat and unwrapped it from around his neck. "Remember that Christmas you made this for me?"

I couldn't imagine Aunt Erma ever knitting anything.

"I can't believe you kept it all these years."

Her voice was high pitched, and she giggled.

My head was spinning. Had she been biding her time all these years? I wanted to run out there and yell at her. How could she do this to me? To the town?

"I always knew we'd do magic together again," he said. They gazed into each other's eyes and stood perfectly still for what felt like an eternity.

Aunt Erma broke the silence. "We're going to do a lot of amazing things." She pulled him into a hug. He said something I couldn't understand, and she giggled again.

I felt sick.

Brenda appeared through the trees and stomped over to Ivan and Aunt Erma. Her presences sucked all the sexual tension out of the woods.

"Quit stalling. I want to get out fo this miserable forest while I still have all my toes," she snapped.

I saw Aunt Erma roll her eyes. "Maybe we should go back this way," she said.

"We've already been that way," someone I couldn't seesaid with a frustrated sigh.

"More IMPs are on their way, and we'll search the entire woods if we have to," Brenda said. I glanced up as though they might descend from the sky. The group disappeared between the trees.

Duncan licked my hand. I knew what I had to do.

I turned and hurried back to the car with Duncan close at my heels.

"We can't let them find the tree," I said when we got back to the car. Duncan wagged his tail in agreement. Aunt Erma derived a lot of power just from harvesting small portions of the tree. The IMPs wouldn't exercise the same restraint once they felt that much magic. The destruction they could do to our magical community was almost unimaginable.

I drove further down the road until I was at the spot closest to the tree. Duncan and I got out of the car. I went around to the trunk and grabbed my tool bag. It always had what I needed. I took a deep breath and marched through the woods.

Along the way I called Violet. She sounded distracted when she picked up.

"You're probably going to want to come find me," I said.

"Why? Where are you?" I had her attention now.

"I'm in the woods, and there's about to be a lot of angry IMPs in here," I said. I did my best to give her directions to my location. I got to the tree. "I have to go. I'll tell you more when you get here." I hung up amid her protests.

Let the chopsticks fall. What Bernie had said made sense now. It always made sense exactly when you needed it to.

I unzipped my tool bag. It was right on top. I don't know how it got there. A shiny axe with a bright red handle. It was smaller than I would have liked, but it would do the job.

I put my hand on the trunk of the tree and felt the tingling rush of magic up my arm. The trunk of the tree began to glow. That was new. Duncan sat solemnly behind me.

"I'm sorry," I whispered to the tree. I shook off the wave of sadness.

Then I swung the axe hard against the trunk. Sparks shot out from the tree, and I jumped back. There wasn't time to be afraid. I swung again and again. It had to be done. I imagined Brenda getting the power from the tree and swung harder. I squinted against the flying chunks of wood and sparks. The sound of the axe echoed through the woods. The IMPs could find me at any moment. The adrenaline coursed through me. I gripped the handle tighter and swung again and again.

I knew the best way to cut down a tree. When I was

in college, I'd had a huge crush on a guy, Luke, from my English Composition course. Luke had competed in lumberjack competitions. I'd been his number one fan for a couple months until I'd realized I would never be anything more than his number one fan. But while I was there I'd picked up a lot of tips on the fastest way to chop down a tree. The universe worked in mysterious ways.

My arms were burning, and sweat was dripping down my back. I threw my coat off and kept chopping. I could feel blisters forming under my gloves. Duncan was walking in circles now. He was on high alert, keeping his eyes open for uninvited guests.

When I was on what felt like my thousandth swing, I vowed that I would start keeping a chainsaw in the trunk of my car. I swallowed the lump in my throat as the glow of the tree began to fade. I paused for a breath. I could barely feel the tingling now. Duncan stretched and yawned as though he wished I would hurry so he could get back to his nap, but he didn't stop watching the surrounding trees.

Duncan began to growl. I started chopping again. I was almost all the way through the trunk.

"Stop," a voice cried. I glanced over. It was Ivan. His hair wasn't slicked back anymore. It stuck out to the sides and hung in his face. He was out of breath. "Get away from the tree."

I froze for a second. His eyes had a dangerous glint.

Brenda, Dennis, Stan, and Aunt Erma all appeared between the trees. Duncan's growling got more vicious.

Brenda yelled something. Was that a spell? Aunt Erma tackled her from behind. She's still on our side, I thought as they both crashed into the snow.

I threw myself at the tree.

"Noooo!" Ivan cried.

As I hit the trunk with my body Brenda managed to screech out one more word.

Suddenly everything went black.

When I came to, I was looking up into Henry's worried eyes.

"Is this a dream?" I asked, reaching towards his face. "Because if it is, it's a good one."

He cracked a small smile, but his brow was still furrowed. "How do you feel?" he asked.

"Like someone knocked me out with a spell." I groaned. "But otherwise fantastic."

I felt something on top of my stomach. It was furry. I looked down, and Duncan was resting his head on me. He was whining softly.

"It's okay, buddy," I said. I moved my arm to pet him, and I felt leaves brush against the back of my hand. The tree was on the ground. I did it! I knocked it over before I passed out. The IMPs wouldn't ever be able to get to the magic now. The trunk wasn't glowing anymore. I reached out to touch the nearest branch. It felt cold against my fingers. Tears pricked in my eyes.

There was some yelling, and I sat up quickly to see what the commotion was all about. I felt woozy.

"Careful." Henry grabbed my shoulders.

Violet, the Morning Pie Crew, and several Magic Enforcement Officers were there detaining the IMPs. Brenda was yelling at Dennis and Stan, and Ivan was yelling at Brenda. From what I could gather, Brenda blamed Dennis and Stan for not finding the tree sooner and Ivan blamed Brenda for scaring away half of their IMP recruits with her off-putting personality.

They were detained in magic handcuffs. They looked like regular handcuffs, but Henry explained that they couldn't do magic while they were wearing them. Stan almost looked relieved to be caught. Maybe magic jail would be a better place for him, as long as he didn't end up in a cell next to his mother.

They were lining up more people in handcuffs. People I didn't recognize.

"Those are other IMPs. They were in the woods looking for this, apparently," Henry said, pointing to the tree. "What exactly is this?"

I told him about the tree. It didn't seem as if I had to keep the secret anymore. "I'm sorry I didn't tell you earlier," I said.

"I understand why you didn't," he said, pulling a twig out of my hair.

I was still sitting on the ground, and Henry was crouching next to me when Aunt Erma walked towards us. My stomach did a flip.

"I'm sorry about your tree," I said.

She crouched down in front of me. "You did exactly what you had to do. You saved us all. If the IMPs had gotten a hold of the tree, it would have been catastrophic," she said firmly.

I looked deep into her eyes, searching for something. Maybe a hint of betrayal. She held my gaze, and I knew. She'd been on my side the whole time we were in the woods.

"I'm very proud of you," she added.

I blinked back tears and nodded.

"Now here, eat this." Aunt Erma handed me a taffy. "It should make you feel better."

I put it in my mouth and the queasy feeling faded. "What exactly is in these?" I asked as I chewed.

She smiled at me. "I still have one or two secrets up my sleeve."

Henry offered to drive me home, and Aunt Erma said she would stay and help Violet.

Once we were in the car, Duncan leaned over the front seat and rested his head on my shoulder. I felt more love for him than I'd ever thought would be possible to feel for a dog.

"Do you think Aunt Erma is capable of doing bad magic?" I asked.

Henry paused for a minute. "I think everyone is capable of doing bad magic," he said.

Exhaustion set in, and the minute we got back to the

apartment I stumbled to the sofa and collapsed. Duncan carefully climbed in next to me. I didn't bother to shoo him out. He opted to be the big spoon. I mumbled goodnight to Henry and was out.

Chapter 18

Dear Elodie,

Over the years I've helped all of my friends move. Some multiple times. Hours of work with nothing but the promise of pizza and beer and their help when I moved.

Well, last week I moved for the first time, and NONE of my friends could help. They all had excuses from feeling sick to being tired to having a hangnail. Yes. Seriously. Is it time for me to get new friends?

Sincerely,
The Loneliest Mover

Dear Loneliest Mover,

It's funny how our friends seem to disappear when we need them the most. People have a tendency to forget about favors they owe. Especially when it comes to moving. You can either be "tired" or suffer from a hangnail next time they need help or you can talk to them and tell them you're frustrated. If talking to them doesn't get anywhere, it might be time to find new friends.

Ask and I'll Answer,

Elodie

I straightened the wreath on the door. I felt the familiar thrill of Christmas run through me. Everyone was coming to my new apartment to celebrate. Duncan and I had moved in a couple days ago. Aunt Erma, my mother, Flora, Lena, Mr. Barnes, Holly and Henry had all helped me move, so it had only taken about five minutes. I didn't have much stuff yet.

I'd gone back to my apartment in the city and sold a lot of my things after it had become apparent that I would be in Hocus Hills for a while. So I was mostly starting from scratch here, and I liked that.

Flora had an old bed I could use, and Lena and I had built a small coffee table out of some of the wood from the magic tree. Aunt Erma had given me lots of twinkle lights to hang around the apartment. I'd found an over-stuffed blue chair at the consignment shop. When I sat in the chair, I felt as if I were sitting in a cloud. That was all the furniture in my apartment so far. So, Christmas was going to be a "bring your own chair" event.

On moving day my mother had brought me a potted plant and a healthy dose of motherly guilt. "Are you sure this apartment is a good idea?" she'd asked. "It's just so ... permanent."

My mother had gotten the gist of what had happened out in the woods. I'd tried to sugar-coat the story for her, avoiding details like Brenda casting a spell on me and just how many IMPs we were up against. Even so, she'd doubled down on her efforts to get me back to the city.

"It's a month-to-month lease, Mom. And yes, I'm sure," I'd said, giving her a hug.

Aunt Erma came early to the celebration, carrying a bottle of champagne. We hadn't had much chance to talk since that day in the woods. I had some questions for her about the things Ivan had said.

"Quite a week we've had." She popped the cork while I stared at the few dishes in my cupboards.

"More exciting than most I've had," I said. I opted for the chipped mugs I'd swiped from the pie shop.

Aunt Erma had brought Mitzy along, and Mitzy was staring intently at Duncan's sleeping body as though she could will him to wake up. When subtlety didn't work, she walked over and stepped on his head. He woke up for a moment, sniffed her, and then went back to sleep. Poor Mitzy. She'd got the short end of the stick when she'd ended up with Duncan as her best friend.

We clinked our mugs and sat down. I sat cross-legged on the bed and Aunt Erma sat in the blue chair.

"I know you've learned some things about my past. Some things I was hoping you'd never find out," she started. I nodded and took a sip of champagne as I waited for her to continue. "Your father was one of my best friends. After he died, your mother forbid me from ever seeing you or her again because she blamed me for not trying to save him with magic."

I nodded again. I'd heard this part before, but I had a feeling she had to ease into the story, for her sake as much as mine.

"I was lost. Everything I'd held onto before, the things that stabilized me, the people who made my life make sense, were gone."

"Did you ever try to talk to Mom again? After Dad died?" I asked.

She nodded sadly. "I tried many times over the years to talk to her, but she always refused to let me back in." She picked a couple dog hairs off the blue chair. "While I don't agree with her decision to cut me out, I know she was in so much pain after your father died. She was lost too." She took a breath. "I was at my lowest point when I met Ivan. He had just lost his sister. We were both looking for a new beginning, and we understood each other in a way I didn't know if I would ever find again."

I stood and refilled both of our mugs with champagne.

"I can't pinpoint exactly when things got out of control. We were both a little bitter and felt like we deserved better. More people joined us. We formed a sort of family, I suppose. The magic we were doing seemed harmless at first. We took some things we wanted. Small stuff. We would control non-magic people for just a few minutes here and there to get our way. To get free drinks or a table at a restaurant. I don't know when it became bigger. It was gradual. Mr. Barnes saved me from that life. The others don't even know about it," she said. "He saw me put a spell on a man, so I could steal his car. The man almost got hit by oncoming traffic when I made him step away from his vehicle." She glanced at me. "I know, not my proudest moment. But Mr. Barnes saved the man and reminded me that I could do good things with my magic. He has a way of making the world sound beautiful and hopeful. He brought me to Hocus Hills. I opened the pie shop and never looked back."

"Didn't Ivan ever come looking for you before now?" I asked.

She shook her head. "I assumed he moved on with his life too. I heard the IMPs still existed, but I hadn't heard from him until his voice was on my answering machine."

"Did you consider going back to the IMPs?" I couldn't look at her when I asked the question, but I needed the answer.

"No," she answered firmly. "They were a mistake from my past. They're not a page from my future."

We finished the bottle of champagne, and with each clink of our mugs came more love and understanding.

Buster Hopkins had called again to see if I'd reconsidered his offer. I'd told him I really appreciated it, but I was going to be in Hocus Hills for the foreseeable future.

The only thing left hanging over my head on Christmas morning was Josh. I hated how we'd ended things, but I pushed that out of my mind, so I could focus on the festivities.

My mother came over to help me make veggie lasagna, mashed potatoes and four kinds of pie.

Once everything was prepared, my mother surveyed our meatless meal and asked if I was sure I was getting enough protein in my diet.

"Yes, Mom." I answered the question for the thousandth time with an audible sigh.

Mr. Barnes arrived with a salad and some candles. "They're made from a mix of essential oils, including lavender, to promote tranquility," he said. I lit them right away.

Lena brought cheese puffs and a bottle of wine. Flora brought a fruit salad and a stack of framed pictures for my walls. She had been making us pose all week, every time we were at the pie shop, and now I knew why. I laughed when I saw the one where Lena had flung a bite of pie at the camera. The camera had caught the moment right before blueberries hit the lens. Everyone except Lena was in the background looking shocked. Lena was laughing hysterically.

Holly and her mother, Luanne, came next. Holly brought chocolates shaped like Santa Claus and Luanne brought something with kale and spinach. She was always critiquing the food I bought at the grocery store and telling me I needed to eat more greens.

Violet arrived looking exhausted, but satisfied, and

carrying a large basket of garlic bread. She told us they had detained several more IMPs, and the rest had gone back underground. We wouldn't be hearing from them for a while.

"What about the people who were thinking about joining the IMPs, but hadn't yet?" I asked. I thought back to the partial conversation I'd overheard on the bobsledding hill.

"We're keeping an eye on them, but we generally find they're more talk that action." I hoped that was true.

She also lectured Aunt Erma and me again on how dangerous it was to be out in the woods with the IMPs without the Magic Enforcement Officers behind us. The first time had been right after the day in the woods. Aunt Erma had argued with Violet, saying that she'd had to go in alone.

"If the IMPs had even gotten a whiff of the Magic Enforcement Officers, things could have gotten really ugly really quickly," Aunt Erma had told her. But Violet wouldn't have any of it.

I took every lecture with a bowed head and a lot of nodding because I didn't see a point in arguing with Violet. I would never win.

She must be in a good mood today. This time she kept her lecture short. I considered that to be her Christmas gift to me.

Henry burst through the door next wearing a Santa hat and carrying a large tray of something covered in powdered sugar in one hand and his guitar in the other. His giant dog, Willy, followed closely behind him. I gave Henry a kiss, and he held up a bag that was wrapped around his wrist.

"Claire sent over some of her special eggnog. Drink at your own risk," he said.

With ten people and two dogs, my new apartment was at capacity, and I loved it. The room was filled with food and cheerful chattering.

There was a knock at the door. Everyone was here. Who could it be? The room quieted, and they all turned toward the door. Clearly, they were wondering the same thing. I opened it, and there was Josh, looking sheepish and uncomfortable.

"Hi," he said. Then he noticed the packed apartment and he shrank back. Everyone was quiet and staring at him.

"Hi," I said with a sigh. I hadn't told anyone besides Henry and Holly exactly what had happened between Josh and me, but they'd clearly picked up enough to know that Josh and I weren't speaking anymore. Flora had asked me the other day when Josh would be coming by again because she had a book she wanted to lend him. I'd said, "Don't know. Don't care." The line of questioning had stopped there.

"Can I talk to you?" he asked quietly. "Please?"

There was no place to talk privately in the apartment, unless we went into the bathroom, which would certainly be one way to make an awkward conversation even more awkward. I stepped out to the hallway, closing the door behind me.

I walked halfway down the hall before stopping. I knew every ear in the apartment would be pressed against my door the second I closed it. I was tempted to throw it open just to watch them all scatter.

"What's up?" I asked after we'd stood for a moment in silence.

"First, I wanted to say I'm sorry," he said.

"Oh? For what?" I wasn't going to let him off the hook that easily.

"For coming here and saying I love you without thinking of the repercussions. I should have told you a long time ago. I had no right coming here and messing with your life. Especially since you seem so happy, and Henry seems like such a stand-up guy," he said.

"Yeah, he is," I said. Josh met my eyes for the first time since we'd gone out to the hallway.

"That became even more apparent when he invited me here today," Josh said.

"He invited you?" I was a little surprised. Wow, Henry really was a stand-up guy.

"I'm also very sorry that I called you selfish. I was hurt, and I lashed out, but that's no excuse. I was the one being selfish. I shouldn't have projected that on you. I put you in a terrible spot and I'm sorry," he said.

"Thank you," I said. "And I forgive you."

"My project is almost done, and I'll be leaving to go back home in a couple days." He paused for a breath. "I don't know how to be your friend when I feel like this. Maybe one day I can find my Henry." He smiled a little. "Or Henrietta."

"I'd like our friendship back," I agreed. "Some day. You should come in for dinner, though," I said. The time apart could start after Christmas dinner.

He smiled. "I'd like that. Thank you."

Everyone's wide, curious eyes stared at us when we walked through the door.

"Josh is going to join us for dinner," I said with a smile, so everyone would know he was forgiven. My mother looked thrilled.

Flora poured Josh a glass of wine, and he slid right into a conversation with Mr. Barnes and Luanne.

Henry followed me as I went to check on the lasagna in the oven.

"Is everything okay?" he asked in a low voice. The chatter had started up again, so we could talk and not be overheard.

"Yes. Thanks for inviting him here so we could patch things up. All feels right with the world now," I said.

"I just wanted to give you this." He pulled a package wrapped in sparkly blue snowflake paper from behind his back.

I smiled at him and unwrapped it. It was a tool belt. Soft, but strong and just the right size. I turned it over in my hands. It was made out of red canvas, just like my tool bag.

"I love it!" I said.

"I thought maybe you could use it when you do projects around town or maybe you'll start a handyman business of your own," he said. "And look." He showed me the inside of the hammer loop. H heart S was embroidered on it in gold thread. It was the perfect gift. I pulled him in for a kiss.

"There's more," he said. He pointed to one of the pouches on the belt. I opened it up and peeked inside. There were two tickets to see the musical *Annie* in the city next month. "I thought we could have a night for just you and me." He kissed me again.

"I love *Annie*." I beamed at him. I also loved the idea of having Henry to myself for a whole evening.

I pulled out my package for him, cringing a little as I thought of the gift inside. I'd put it in an Erma's Pie Shop box and tied a silver ribbon around it. He opened the box and lit up. "I love it! In fact, I'm going to wear it right now." He pulled off the shirt he was wearing and put the sweater on.

Holly hadn't been as kind as Flora when I'd shown her the blue sweater I'd planned on giving to Henry. She scoffed-shook her head and said I needed to do better for our first Christmas together. She'd helped me personalize it by sewing a fabric version of Henry's dog, Willy, on the front. I'd offered little help, but lots of encouragement throughout the project. Luckily, I'd been able to avoid her offer to include my likeness on the sweater too.

I stepped back to admire Henry in the sweater for a moment. He was particularly adorable with his hair sticking out in all directions after pulling on the sweater. I couldn't help but smile at the way he looked at me. I was pretty sure I had the same gooey look on my face.

Maybe one day I would get better at gift-giving, but I also hoped it would always be Henry I was giving the gifts to.

Mr. Barnes began singing "Deck the Halls". Henry pulled out his guitar and strummed along. Soon everyone was singing. I tried to blink back my happy tears. I felt so lucky to be a part of this big strange family.

I went to sleep happy that night. I could still feel the warm glow of love and wine. Duncan was snuggled into my back. It would be nice if he didn't snore so loudly. I moved my head a little further from his mouth and drifted off into a deep sleep.

I sat straight up in bed. Duncan reluctantly lifted his head to look at me. I didn't know how long I had been asleep. I must have been dreaming, but it was so vivid. I put on my boots and coat. Duncan followed me, his tail wagging.

"Are you coming with?" I asked, a little surprised. I thought he would prefer to stay in the cozy bed. His tail wagged harder, so I grabbed his leash.

It was dark and cold outside. I could hear the wind chimes in front of Flora's shop softly jingling in the breeze.

I cringed a little as I started my car. I really should get my muffler fixed.

It was still clear in my mind. Usually my dreams, even the ones I tried to remember, faded quickly after I got up. Not this time. It was as though my mind was giving me step-by-step directions. "Turn left in three hundred feet. Turn right at the stoplight. Merge onto the highway." I exited the highway and drove down an asphalt road. The asphalt road turned into a dirt road. The trees got thicker. "Stop," the GPS in my mind said. Duncan and I got out of the car and walked into the woods. The air was quiet except for a few leaves rustling and our feet crunching in the snow.

"We're here," I whispered and dropped to my knees. Duncan crept up slowly behind me. He sniffed the air, but lost interest when he didn't see any food. I gently dug the snow away. There it was. It was small, just a twig sticking out of the ground with a few tiny green leaves growing out of it.

"Hey, friend," I whispered. I pulled off my mitten and gently touched one of the leaves. I could feel the tingle of magic.

THE END

Acknowledgements

A huge thank you to my wonderful editor, Charlotte Ledger, and the whole amazing team at One More Chapter! Working with you is a dream come true for me!

I'm lucky to have the brilliant Char Torkelson in my life. You've taught me so much about writing, and your cheerleading has helped me bulldoze through my doubts and keep going.

I love Mondays thanks to my Monday night writing group. Marilyn, Anne, Susan, Fay, Charissa, Patty, and Jim – you inspire me every week with your stories and feedback.

To my parents, Richard and Sheila, and my brother, Daniel. I'm grateful for all your love and support. Thank you for making Christmas a magical time filled with laughter and remote control helicopter competitions. Love you guys!

Thank you to my husband, Chris, who is always ready for emergency ice cream or taco runs and who never fails to provide a dose of encouragement when I need it the most. Love you!

To my dogs, Bella and Chloe, thank you for your daily reminders to snuggle, play, and dance before dinner. Chloe, we may not have found each other near a magic tree, but your presence in my life certainly was magical. I miss you every day.